RED MAN RISING

RED MAN RISING

By Darren Lamica

All of men's competency is derived from their burden of performance. Women just are; men must become.
  —Rollo Tomassi

CONTENTS

CHAPTER 1

The cool air and darkness of night produced a calmness and sense of peace. A steady breeze, with the occasional whispers of his men, interrupted the silence surrounding Sergeant John Deveraux. He looked up at the starlit sky, enamored with its beauty. He closed his eyes and took in a deep breath, savoring a moment's peace. This was the first time he had felt a sense of calmness in the last few days.

He began to think about his girlfriend, Susan Williams, who lived ten thousand miles away in Alabama, how it seemed like an eternity ago that he had been with her. His heart began to feel a sense of ache as he hoped that she was safe and that he would be with her soon. His thoughts drifted away; he pondered his return to the States. His goal was to marry Susan and raise a family, something John wanted very much. He also wanted his children to grow up safe and happy, unlike how he had been raised.

GROWING UP

John had grown up very poor in a small town in upstate New York. His town was like many small towns across America. It happened to be so far north along the border of Canada that it could be overlooked on any map, only found by those from there or passing through; it was the perfect place to raise a family—one exception being the harsh winters that seemed to take up six months of the year.

John and his family lived in a decrepit trailer, which had exterior plywood walls and insulation showing in the interior. Rooms were separated by blanket dividers and several types of uneven flooring. Winters were especially harsh because the trailer was only heated by a woodstove. It seemed there were never enough blankets to keep him warm at night.

As he was raised in this environment, John was able to acclimate to the harsh cold and periodic lack of food. His stepfather, Robert Devereaux, worked for a road maintenance crew the next town over, while his mother, Linda Devereaux, was a stay-at-home mother. Linda had married Robert shortly after leaving John and his older sister Savanah's biological father because of his excessive dependence on alcohol. The nightly beatings of Linda and young John became too much for Linda to bear; Savanah seemed to be the only safe one in the house.

By all outward appearances, Robert was a great stepfather. He taught John how to hunt, fish, and raise a garden to supplement what they could not buy in the supermarket—basic things to survive and be self-reliant. John was taught how to work on vehicles and repair things when they broke. There was no extra money in the family budget to hire someone to address any problems that arose.

John's other responsibilities were to make sure the wood was split and brought into the house every evening. During the winter, he shoveled the driveway, while in the spring and summer he cut and split wood, ensuring there was enough to last the winter. When John turned eleven, he worked on a farm picking stones, tending to the cattle, cleaning the barn, and performing whatever other chores the farmer assigned him. Every week John would turn over his paycheck to his parents, as they needed the money for food and to keep the lights on.

Robert explained to John that turning over his paychecks was for the best of the family. John was conditioned to believe that when he became a husband and father, it would be his duty to provide for the family. His wife and kids always would come first. He, as the "man," would be expected to be selfless and do what was always best for them, even if it came at a personal sacrifice. "Women and children first" was ingrained into his young mind.

As John grew up, that mind-set became imprinted further. Robert cemented those teachings in his relationships with Linda and Savanah. It was during this time that Robert's growing dependence on alcohol began to show its effects. Robert would drink heavily after work to numb himself to the day's stresses, further exacerbating the decline in his relationship with Linda. Some nights Robert would sit in his recliner, bottle in hand, and watch TV.

Other nights Robert would become enraged out of nowhere and begin verbally abusing John. Robert was disappointed in John for not being stronger, smarter—or for whatever other perceived inadequacies. John thought he was never good enough and could never measure up to Robert's expectations. John would continually try to please him and Linda by acquiescing to whatever he was told. Robert always seemed to protect Savanah and never ridiculed her harshly as he did John.

Internally Robert resented John for not being his biological son. He resented providing for a son and daughter that were not his own blood. He resented his job, his wife, and all that he perceived as life happening to him. Life always *happened* to him, and he felt he had no control. The best escape for him was to a bottle, where he would numb his mind and his internal struggles.

It was this escape that he looked forward to at every chance. Robert knew the burden of performance was on him to provide for the family. It was his duty to ensure there was food in the home and a roof over his family's head. This always weighed heavily on him. If he did not perform, the family would suffer. In dealing with these suppressed emotions, Robert had occasional outbursts directed at John. He considered John a boy and thought he should be taught to be a man.

These lessons on being a man not only included being head of the house but also included being responsible for the whole family. To be considered a man, John needed to be tough enough to take a hit. The beatings began soon after. Initially it started with a slap on the face or the whip of a belt. Over time the beatings became more intense. Slaps turned into punches, belt and paddle hits turned into welts and severe bruising. The beatings culminated in one evening during which Robert grabbed John and pushed him into an exposed two-by-four.

John's head hit the edge of the two-by-four with such force that his forehead split in the center. John fell to the ground, his body appearing lifeless. When he woke up, still in a daze, he felt a bandage wrapped around his head as he lay in bed. He didn't know where he was until his mother opened the blanket to check on him.

She asked John, "Are you all right? You tripped really hard and hit your head."

John replied, "I don't remember anything after hitting my head."

Linda responded, "You hit your head really hard, and I had to sew it up. It's only a couple stitches, and you will be fine. You're a tough young man, and you will be OK."

John replied, "But it hurts so much."

Linda said in a stern tone of voice, "You need to act like a man. Men don't complain about such things." She continued, "When you go to school on Monday, if anyone asks, you were working in the woods with Robert cutting trees down, and a branch hit you on the head. If anyone asks you any further questions, do not answer them; teachers can talk to us if they have any questions."

John replied, "Yes, ma'am; I won't say anything."

Linda replied, "Good boy. Now rest, and I'll be back in a little bit to check on you."

John remembered exactly what had happened the night before. He also thought it was his duty to protect his father. Should anyone find out the truth, Robert would go to jail and would lose his job. The family would lose everything, and there would be no money to take care of Linda. Family always comes first, and sometimes you have to make sacrifices, even at your own expense. It was John's conditioning to accept this as his responsibility so he could show Robert he was a man. No word was ever mentioned about the truth of that night, but it remained forever vivid in John's mind.

It was also in John's conditioning that men should be not only selfless and protectors of women and children but also strong like a rock. "Men" did not outwardly express any emotions of pain or displeasure. Robert explained that when a man expressed emotions of sadness or displeasure or cried around women, it made women feel uncomfortable.

It was men's responsibility to make sure they were aware of women's feelings. Men should not intentionally upset them. Women needed protection and security. Men were responsible for making sure they were always comfortable. This was, John reasoned, the reason that his sister Savanah never bore the brunt of Robert's abuse, why he took the beatings and Robert never laid a finger on her.

When Monday came around, there were of course many probing questions by students and faculty. John did as he was told and explained the same story his mother had outlined for him. When pressed further, John told his teachers to go to his parents with any additional questions; his mind was still hazy from the incident.

Nothing came of the incident, and life continued. Beatings were becoming a nearly nightly occurrence for John. Robert was careful this time to not leave any marks that would provoke questions. John's emotional state had begun to crack from the excessive abuse, but in his mind, he thought he was being toughened up to be a man.

In school John was academically average as a student. Much of the work and abuse at home distracted him from his studies, and his grades were a direct reflection of that. Although a very good-looking young man with brown hair and brown eyes, John was very small framed at five foot seven and 120 pounds soaking wet; he was self-conscious about the scar on his forehead and socially awkward with his classmates, who considered him a loner.

John was often withdrawn, with no real friends he could talk to. He always kept his problems to himself. That's what men do. As a smaller-framed young man, with biannual haircuts and less-than-fashionable clothing, John was a prime target for bullies. Bullies were merciless with John; he would get pushed around the halls, tripped, openly mocked, and degraded in any number of other ways.

As John was walking into his eighth-grade homeroom one day, one of the students tripped him, and he fell hard on the floor. His books spread across the floor in every direction. He hit the surface so hard that part of the bone in his elbow apparently chipped. He was in a lot of pain. John's internalized emotions were released beyond his control as he began to cry. The whole class burst into laughter as John lay on the ground, crying even harder out of pain and embarrassment. It was then that Ms. Baker, the homeroom teacher, came in to find the scene unfolding before her.

Curtly, she asked, "What happened to John?" as she knelt to help him. No student responded, all still silently giggling.

"Who's responsible for this?" she asked sternly.

One of the students chimed in, "He just walked into class and tripped, Ms. Baker."

Ms. Baker helped John up and escorted him to the nurse's office, along the way asking what had happened.

"I tripped," replied John, still self-aware enough not to reveal the identities of the real culprits.

Lying in the nurse's office, dried tears on his face, he questioned why the world was against him. He hadn't done anything wrong. It was then John came up with a plan to make it stop. He was going to put an end to the abuse from Robert and the bullies at school. *My plan will work*, he thought. *It's the best solution.* As he lay on the nurse's office bed, his bruised elbow aching, John began to devise his plan. He was going to get back at everyone who had ever hurt him. *It has to work*, he reasoned with himself.

When John returned home after a long day at school, his sister having stayed after school, he got off the bus and walked into the trailer. His parents were not home, and he thought to himself, *This is the perfect time to carry out my plan.* He set down his bookbag on the table and walked into his parents' bedroom. At thirteen years old, he already knew how to handle a gun. Robert had shown him many times while target shooting and hunting. He took his mother's .30–30 Winchester off the open gun rack and laid it on his parent's bed. Opening the drawer, he took out the appropriate box of ammunition. With one single shell, he loaded the rifle, tears beginning to fill his eyes.

His thoughts were racing. *Everyone will be so sorry they ever hurt me. I will never feel pain again. Everyone will forget I ever existed. Nobody even cares about me; God doesn't even care about me—if he did, he would help me. It's better if I die so I don't feel any more pain.* Resting the butt of the rifle on the ground, the barrel aimed at his face, John was moments away from pulling the trigger. Like Robert, John's reality centered on why everything always happened to him. John asked himself two final questions: *Why do bad things always happen to me? Why is everyone out to get me?*

Somewhere within his subconscious, he heard an answer—*Because you let them happen.* Suddenly everything made perfect sense to John. He was responsible for how people treated him. Life wasn't happening to him; life was happening because he allowed life to happen to him. This hit him like a ton of bricks. Something changed deep inside John that day. No longer was he going to accept this treatment from anyone.

He wasn't going to get bullied any longer, and that included the abuse from Robert. He was in charge of his life; life was not in charge of him. Burning rage and resolve began to fill his insides. He had to come up with a plan to change everything around, but how?

With this new resolve, John wanted to live. He unloaded his mother's rifle and cleaned away any possible fingerprints he may have left. He returned the shells and rifle to the gun rack. Mentally and emotionally drained, he lay down on his bed and quickly fell asleep.

Many men can remember a time where they have been "zeroed" out. It's the time where all hope seems lost and one feels the desperation of not having a clearly defined way forward. What John felt was absolute desperation in a situation he was thankfully able to recover from. Although the mental scarring was already imprinted in him, John knew he had to move forward—even when his reality told him the situation was hopeless.

John had wanted to be a Marine since he was four years old. His grandfather, a Marine during World War II, had survived some of the Marine Corps' bloodiest battles. He was John's hero. John looked up to him as a man of respect, dignity, and courage as he learned about his grandfather's exploits. John's dream of becoming a Marine like his grandfather made his imagination wild with all the possibilities of what he would experience. The physical and psychological damage that had already been inflicted on John was imprinted on his young thirteen-year-old mind. Not many young boys want to go to war and die on the battlefield, but John certainly did.

John opened his eyes and realized what he had to do. His mission was to leave New York and become a US Marine. Sadly, John could not enlist until he was seventeen years old. He had at least four more years of hell to deal with before he could realize his dream. His plan began solidifying when suddenly Robert opened the curtain and scorned him for leaving his book bag on the table.

"Did you do your homework?" he asked.

John replied, "I was tripped at school today and hurt my elbow, so I took a nap when I got home, sir."

John didn't see the hard fist before it hit his chest.

"Get up, you lazy son of a bitch. The school called us and told us what happened. You cried like a bitch, didn't you?"

John's initial reaction was to plead with Robert and say he wouldn't do it again. Remembering what had happened earlier, that he had nearly killed himself, John felt again the internal resolve he had felt before going to sleep.

"Yes, I cried, and I will no longer cry over how I am treated or how you treat me!" Robert was taken back by John's response. John was standing up for himself for the first time.

"Good, don't let it happen again," he said, smiling, before slapping John on the face. "That's so you remember it."

John felt a strength in himself for the first time in his life as he stood his ground against his stepfather. He got out of bed and walked to the table to do his homework.

Linda asked, "Did anything happen at school today?"

John replied, "I was tripped and cried like a bitch in front of the whole class. But it's OK; I won't cry again."

"Good, because men don't cry, John," his mother responded. Thus John had learned from a young age to suppress his emotions; crying indicated weakness.

After homework was completed and John had sat down at dinner, Linda asked, "John, are you OK? You seem different."

John responded, "I'm OK, Mom. I have been thinking of joining the Marines."

Linda was surprised by John's words. "What do you mean 'joining the Marines'?" she responded.

Robert interrupted, "Marines are pussies who cannot hack it in the real world. Right, soldier boy?"

Calmly, John responded, "Grandpa was a Marine, and he's no pussy."

Robert raised his hand and said there would be no talk like that out of John's mouth.

John retorted, "Yes, sir, but I was just following your example on what you thought of them."

Robert lowered his hand and laughed. "You're not a man yet, so you can't say those words," he chided. "What makes you think you have what it takes to be in the military? You're just a scrawny runt!" He laughed.

With his newfound confidence, John responded, "So make me stronger, sir."

In all of John's years, he had never seen Robert surprised by his responses. Robert felt challenged and accepted John's proposal.

"OK, I hope you're ready," he replied.

Robert had no military experience and was obese. John seemed kind of wary of what was in store for him, but whatever it was, if it didn't kill him, it would make him stronger.

Linda interjected, "We have some news to tell you, John—you're going to be a big brother!"

John sat there quietly as Linda told him he was going to have a sister.

John replied, "That's great; I would love a little sister!"

Robert appeared to be somewhat sad they were having a girl, although he already had two sons from a previous marriage whom he had not seen or spoken to in years.

"Do you have a name?" John replied.

"Julie," Linda answered. After dinner concluded and all the big news had been discussed, John went to bed. He wanted to work on his plan of escape.

Lying in bed, John thought carefully about how he was going to escape his life. It wasn't an overnight fix but something he had to plan over the long term. Joining the Marines was his mission. The question being, how was he going to get there now, being only thirteen? First, he knew he had to graduate high school to join. Second, he knew he had to get stronger mentally and physically. Third, how was he going to deal with the kids at school? So many questions for his young mind to ponder at one time.

The main question was what steps he had to take to be a Marine. Eighth grade was ending soon, and his work at the farm in the summer was going to consist of long, hard days in the field and the barn. John decided the time had come for him to start gaining strength and endurance. He had to be physically fit to endure the rigors of Marine Corps recruit training. He was going to use working on the farm as a means of gaining strength and join the running club to increase endurance and work on his academics. His goal was to graduate early and join the Marines on his seventeenth birthday.

The summer was mostly uneventful as John put in long hours at the farm and ran every chance he could. He didn't have access to any books; the only library in town was at his school. Being poor, he didn't have access to the internet outside of school. But John was becoming stronger and faster.

His dedication and resolve were just as strong as on the night he had decided he was going to be a US Marine. The regular beatings continued every month when the phone bill arrived in the mail. John was accused of calling 1-900 sex line phone numbers, with the result that the phone bill was a couple hundred dollars. No matter how much he protested and pleaded his innocence to his parents, the beatings continued.

This was John's existence; he dreaded every time the phone bill came at the end of the month. Even when school started again, he worried about this eventuality. John often wondered how hard he was going to be beaten and what other punishments would be in store for him when he got home.

Fear turned to acceptance, as John knew he had no control over the phone bill. He could only control how he reacted to the situation and the beatings as they happened. John continued to focus on his physical fitness in the school gym, joined a running club to learn to be a better runner, and attended to his studies; his grades steadily improved.

When John entered the ninth grade, he decided to use all his study halls to take extra classes. While other students used their study halls to study, gossip, or play games, John enrolled in both ninth- and tenth-grade classes, his mind focused on graduating as soon as possible. It wasn't long afterward that school gossip spread about John wanting to join the Marines.

In typical fashion the bullies at school wasted no time in exploiting this new information. John was often teased and harassed. He heard "You'll never make it," "You're too small to be a Marine," and other disparaging comments. John's resolve still unshaken, he ignored their comments and focused on his mission.

Just after the new year, halfway through school, Linda gave birth to Julie. Everything seemed to calm down at home. All of Robert and Linda's attention was focused on Julie. The 1-900 phone sex calls seemed to have stopped completely, and John was no longer being beaten on a regular basis. John was thankful to be almost invisible in his family. This allowed him to continue focusing and improving himself. Being invisible gave John the opportunity to work on his academics at home; his grades were now mostly As.

John was noticeably gaining muscle from the hard work he was putting in at the school gym. Female classmates would comment on how great he was looking. Bullying was almost nonexistent at this point, and everything seemed to be moving in a positive direction for John. Although he mentally considered himself an outcast, John was in fact a social loner. He wanted nothing to do with people and did not want to socially engage with anyone. He could never forget how he was treated in school and at home. He gave no fucks about what people thought about him—besides, after it was all said and done, their opinions didn't matter one bit.

The mental and emotional abuse irreversibly changed John's empathy for other people. John was dead inside. In his mind, he wanted to be a Marine so he would have the chance to die "gloriously" on the battlefield. John never saw a future in which he grew old, and he was fine with that. He wanted to die in a hail of gunfire, ending his internal pain while dying a hero's death. John accepted this as his fate and welcomed the opportunity should it present himself. In his mind, he had already died; it was just a matter of it becoming a reality. Dead man walking.

During the next school year, John would take the requisite tenth- and eleventh-grade courses, although still technically in tenth grade; he would take both eleventh- and twelfth-grade classes in eleventh grade. John was finally going to accomplish his goal and was projected to graduate high school at the age of sixteen. He graduated so young that he had to wait three months after graduation before he could join the Marines. He enlisted in the Marines on his seventeenth birthday.

Home life seemed to improve as well. John was no longer being abused. His stepsister Julie was growing up and was treated like a princess; she was even favored over Savanah. She could never do any wrong, and that was fine with John because at least there was no attention on him. Robert continued drinking; Linda remained a dutiful housewife. Savanah just existed in the house as Julie remained spoiled for attention.

High school graduation day came at last. John graduated with honors a year ahead of his classmates, even becoming a member of the National Honor Society. His first goal accomplished. High school was now in the past as he continued to prepare for his future. John decided he wanted to be an infantryman when he enlisted in the Marines. His grandfather had been an infantry Marine. He wanted to be on the front lines and get his first taste of combat. John watched too many war movies and envisioned himself being a war hero.

Three months of summer flew by as John continued to ready his body and mind in anticipation of recruit training. He was ready to face any challenges that awaited him at boot camp. He was not going to fail. After what seemed like an eternity, John's birthday finally arrived.

Turning seventeen, John was now able to join the Marines—with parental consent, of course. The only birthday gift he wished for was his parents' willingness to sign the papers that allowed him to enlist. His wish was granted—John saw his biological father, a former sailor in the Navy, for the first time in years. John had only visited his father two times in the past, the last visit having taken place nearly ten years ago.

John's father asked, "Are you sure you want to do this? The Marines are very tough. Are you ready for this kind of training?"

John responded, "I've never been more ready in my whole life."

Grabbing a pen from the recruiter, John's father signed the parental consent. It was official: John had enlisted in the Marines on his seventeenth birthday. He had taken the first step to realizing his dream. Shortly thereafter John swore his final oath of enlistment in Albany, New York.

RECRUIT TRAINING

Three weeks later, having just arrived in the early morning hours, John was standing on the infamous yellow footprints at Marine Corps Recruit Training Depot, Parris Island, South Carolina. Marine drill instructors were barking orders loudly, while all of the recruits stared straight ahead with a sense of fear of the unknown.

The shouting was soon followed by chaos as the recruits were ordered to run into the receiving facility and await further instructions. No recruit dared to speak and thus face the wrath of the drill instructors. Each task was completed quickly. Administrative paperwork was processed, heads shaved to create uniformity, uniform and equipment issued—the indoctrination process into being a Marine had begun.

John was assigned to 3rd Recruit Training Battalion, Mike Company, Platoon 3000. Recruit training was about to begin. Having seen the movie *Full Metal Jacket* a hundred times, John expected the worst and hoped for the best. The opening scene from the movie depicted recruit training. Suffice it to say, the movie was very much like the scene before him. John felt mentally prepared for the worst. Thankfully it was not as intense as Hollywood had portrayed.

The first day of training had John standing tall alongside sixty-plus other men. Standing barefoot on a dark-red floor between two thick black lines at the edge of his bunk, the walls heavily coated in an off-white paint, John stared straight ahead, focused on nothing.

He was still drowsy from waking up as orders and directions were barked by five drill instructors walking up and down the two rows of men facing each other. Chaos, confusion, strict obedience to orders—all things that can only be felt and experienced in person.

Recruits were not allowed to look their drill instructors in the eyes, lest they face severe punishment on the quarterdeck. The quarterdeck was used to give recruits additional physical training if they made a mistake. If their rack mates made a mistake, or they needed extra motivation to fall in line with the other recruits, or just for the hell of it, off to the quarterdeck they went. There was no "I," as all individuality was stripped from them the moment of their first haircut in receiving.

Steeped heavily in tradition and a rich history that includes some of America's most iconic battles, the Marine Corps maintains a legendary status as one of the world's finest fighting forces and draws many young men from across the country, all yearning to be a part of such an elite organization. Refined over hundreds of years, recruit training is an indoctrination process that takes young civilian men and women and transforms them into

Marines. What is not typically said is that the indoctrination process lasts in the minds of Marines for a lifetime. One is forever changed and reborn.

Recruit training was all John had anticipated it would be and then some, although his only frame of reference was the Hollywood movies he had watched as a child. Disciplined, organized, and having been exposed to something intensely hard, John felt a sense of camaraderie he had never experienced before. The training was turning John from a civilian into a war fighter. The Marine Corps wants killers, plain and simple.

John did not miss home and received the occasional letter from his family, but he was thankful to be away from them. The Marine Corps was his new family; for all intents and purposes, he was free to start a new chapter in his life, one that would not include Robert and Linda.

Marine recruit training is highly structured. Every minute of the day and every element of training serves a crucial purpose. This is due to the fact the Marine Corps only has thirteen weeks to train civilians into combat-ready, killing Marines. John and the other recruits became accustomed to the routine of waking up at zero dark early, their beds (racks) made tightly and squared away in a timely manner.

There was no time to enjoy a meal, also known as "chow." Everything was made into a sandwich and eaten in silence as quickly as possible. His ability to train hard, his good hygiene, and his strict obedience to orders helped keep the drill instructors from harassing John too much.

In fact, he was doing so well that the instructors had assigned him to be a team leader within the platoon.

Training progressed into the third and final phase of training. John, a stellar recruit, stood out as a high performer within the platoon. Looking back, John realized how fast the last twelve weeks had gone by. He was days away from fulfilling his dream of being a US Marine. The final test he had to complete was the Crucible, the culmination of recruit training.

The Crucible consists of over fifty-four hours of mental, physical, and moral stressors. This includes over forty-five miles of marching and sleep and food depravation as one navigates a barrage of daily and nightly obstacles—assault courses, leadership exercises, and team-building stations. Each obstacle requires recruits to work together as a team, reinforcing Corps values of honor, courage, and commitment.

Camaraderie and teamwork are mind-sets drilled into every recruit from day one. It is essential for recruits to conquer the Crucible. It is *the* rite of passage every Marine must undergo in order to earn their eagle, globe, and anchor (EGA) along with the forever title "US Marine."

Sleep deprived, starving, and physically drained, John was just hours from completing the last challenge of the Crucible. Only a nine-mile road march back to the main parade deck at Parris Island remained. As night turned into dawn, the recruits continued marching. Every step forward was one step closer to the finish.

The thought of quitting never entered his mind; he couldn't quit now that he was so close. John thought about his childhood, school, and the training he had been through. A sense of pride and newfound energy kept him focused and driven to finish the march.

The young recruits finish the nine-mile road march and stand in formation around a half-sized replica of the Marine Corps Memorial, also known as the Iwo Jima Memorial. A small ceremony takes place as the chaplain reads a prayer and the company first sergeant addresses the recruits. Soon after, platoon drill instructors present each recruit with the Marine Corps insignia. Sweaty, sleep deprived, and with tears streaming down his face, John was handed the Marine Corps insignia and addressed for the first time as "Marine."

The overwhelming sense of pride John felt was like nothing he had ever experienced in his whole life. Everything he had worked so hard for culminated in this very moment. He was a US Marine. Having completed recruit training and the Crucible, having earned the title of Marine, John felt like a man for the first time.

Many boys today in our American society are not given a ritual of passage when they transition from boyhood to manhood. Women and children are valued simply for existing, and this is why the transition to manhood is a rough one for boys. They are no longer loved for simply existing. Young men's worthiness must be proven, or they are nothing. In this one moment, John took his first step into mentally transitioning from a boy to a man—no matter what his father or what other people said or thought.

John thought to himself, *Boys don't experience the same rite of passage as girls, who begin their menstrual cycle and are thus considered women. We are not given that vital transition from boyhood to manhood, and it does us a great disservice.* He vowed that when he had a son of his own one day, he would make sure he had that special moment of tribulation and transition of which John had been deprived.

Graduation day came in the middle of January. John, dressed sharply in his Marine Corps uniform, marched with pride across the cold parade deck, with the families of the new Marines seated in the stands and all looking for their loved ones amid the sea of uniforms. John wore a new stripe on his sleeve; he had been meritoriously promoted to Private First Class (PFC). John's senior drill instructor had promoted him for his hard work and dedication as a team leader during recruit training. John's graduation officially made him a Marine—a title that cannot be taken, given, or bought. It is a title that would remain with him for the rest of his life.

MILITARY LIFE

After graduation and an extended period of leave, John reported to the Infantry Training Battalion (ITB) located at Camp Geiger, a satellite facility of Camp Lejeune in North Carolina. During his leave, John had spent time with his family in New York but couldn't wait to get back into training. Robert and Linda had treated John differently. There had been a sense of respect in how Robert treated John. Robert, never having served in the military, had seen incredible strength in John for having completed basic training.

Although this fact was unspoken, Robert and Linda had come to respect John for his strength and mental fortitude. He was no longer seen or talked to like a boy but rather like a man. Though indifferent to this fact, John was a changed man. He was no longer the boy who had left, and his parents could see the drastic change. He was no longer quiet and demure, a pushover. There was a sense of cockiness, confidence, steadfastness, and strength his parents had never seen.

Reporting as ordered, John began his two-month infantry training course. The course turns those who have completed basic training into combat-effective Marines—offering the knowledge and skills to fight on the battlefield and the honing of killer instincts. The potential and propensity for violence scares the shit out of men. The Marine Corps embraces that potential for future use on the battlefield.

A warrior is no good on the battlefield if he does not have a propensity for violence. Hence the phrase "It's better to be a warrior in the garden than a gardener in a war." A man who does not have a propensity for violence is not a peaceful man. He is harmless. A man capable of extreme violence, however, *chooses* to be peaceful.

Having no sense of emotional connection or empathy for other people due to his abusive childhood made it easier for John to transition from civilian to Marine. For the first time in his life, John felt like he was a part of something much bigger than himself. He belonged to an organization heavy in tradition and legendary status on the battlefield as one of the world's finest fighting forces.

He excelled in the infantry training course and absorbed as much of the course material and training as he could.

He wanted to be a lethal instrument of death, honing his skills to be the best warrior and Marine he could be. Upon graduation from infantry training, John was meritoriously promoted to Lance Corporal by the training command, due in part to his having excelled in training both academically and in the field. John's childhood had suppressed the natural leader instincts within him; the Marine Corps brought out his natural characteristics as John adapted to his new life. His commands during recruit and infantry training quickly realized his potential.

At the conclusion of infantry training, John received orders after graduation to report to 1st Battalion, 8th Marines, 2nd Marine Division (1/8) located at Camp Lejeune. John was a bit apprehensive as he did not know what to expect when he hit the Fleet Marine Force (FMF).

Basic and advanced training were complete. Now he was about to join a real infantry unit that could deploy anywhere around the world. He had also heard intense stories of how new Marines, nicknamed "boots," were hazed upon joining their first unit. Hazing is another rite of passage young Marines must endure in order to be accepted into their first new unit. It's about the establishment of dominance and a willingness to obey orders of "salty Marines" (Marines who have served at least one deployment in the FMF). This ensures that boots are keenly aware of where they stand in the pecking order. Any deviance from this is severely punished through additional hazing and military instruction.

Although hazing is not typically personal, sometimes it is the best way to straighten out a Marine if he has fucked up. This prevents paperwork, which could ruin his future career. Most Marines would rather be hazed than have paperwork done on them, full stop. Nobody wants a paper trail. Typically, once the initial hazing period is over, boots who have proven themselves are welcomed into the unit as a member of the team. There are always exceptions to every rule, of course.

The bus transporting John to Camp Lejeune from Camp Geiger came to a stop in the parking lot outside of the barracks to 1/8. The Marines off-loaded the bus and were directed to stand in formation in the parking lot. There they received further instructions from a handful of senior noncommissioned officers (SNCO) and noncommissioned officers (NCO) from each company—Alpha, Bravo, and Charlie.

Within each company the young Marines were divided up and placed into one of three platoons—first, second, or third. From there they were sectioned off into one of three squads, each comprising about twelve Marines, and into fireteams, each comprising about four Marines. Everything was very organized and structured (that at least is the initial thought when one has no prior experience). The SNCOs and NCOs of the respective companies looked at the new boots as if they were about to receive a new toy to play with.

The Marines were divided off between the companies and platoons. John was placed in Alpha Company, First Platoon, First Squad, Third Fireteam. Let the games begin, as they say. Once John and the other Marines were assigned to their respective units, the NCOs wasted no time in barking orders like drill instructors.

Mass chaos ensued as John and several Marines tried to gather their gear and run to their new barracks room. This was going to be a long day, and it was just beginning. It seemed to him the easiest part of being a Marine was recruit training. Little did John realize how accurate his assessment was.

John remained awake all night, as he was forced to clean his barracks room, also known as "Chinese field day," during which every piece of furniture is taken out of the room and placed on the balcony. Every nook and corner is cleaned to Q-tip and white-glove standards. If the room is not satisfactorily cleaned, the Marines have to remove the furniture and start over again. It's a long, mundane process that makes all Marines want to move out of the barracks.

Amid the push-ups, punches, pushing, and berating talk, John kept his mouth shut and did what was expected of him. Like he had in boot camp and infantry training, he did what he was told as quickly as possible and followed the directions given to him. Keeping a low profile as a boot in the Marines is vital to surviving the first few months in the fleet. Just do what you're told, when you're told, and accomplish your task immediately. Also, don't walk on the grass.

CHAPTER 2

F ast-forward to the invasion of Iraq in 2003: Gunfire began to erupt in the dead of night. John's squad began to return heavy suppressive fire on the enemy combatants, snapping him out of his thoughts, as they remained dug into their fighting positions in the cold Iraqi dessert.

The invasion of Iraq had begun a few days prior, and the only casualties inflicted thus far had been on enemy Iraqi troops and militia loyal to the Hussein regime. The reality of war was about to change the life of Sergeant Devereaux forever.

As bullets began to sporadically impact the dirt around John and his squad, there was no sense of fear of death. There wasn't time to think, only to react to the situation as it unfolded. In the Marine Corps, muscle memory is a powerful tool for anyone who wishes to perform well when the pressure is on, especially in a combat situation where there is a high propensity for confusion—"fog of war"—sheer violence, and lots of blood. There is the very real possibility of facing your own death.

In these highly stressful environments, training auto-matically suppresses natural human reactions of tunnel vison and fear as you start doing things without even thinking about them, amazingly.

The sporadic gunfire ceased just as quickly as it had started. Using his night vision goggles (NVGs), John sur-veyed the area in front of him. All he saw was a barren dessert with a couple dead enemy combatants lying on the ground, motionless. John had left Kuwait only a few days prior, and this was the first real combat and death he and his squad had experienced thus far in the invasion.

Moving out of his fighting position, John began to check on the status of his squad to ensure there were no casualties. He made sure his men had enough ammuni-tion ready to go in case there was another attack. John's squad had thankfully incurred no casualties. However, in Second Squad, one Marine, an eighteen-year-old PFC just out of training and only two months into 3/2, had taken a round to the head. He was killed instantly.

After checking on his men, John went over to Second Squad's dug-in location. The platoon commander, Lieutenant. Mike Smith, and Staff Sergeant Frank Steele were already surrounding the dead Marine. The Navy corpsman, affectionately known as "doc," along with the squad leaders of Second and Third Squads, stood over his lifeless body.

John saw the young Marine's lifeless, bloody body on the ground, a bullet hole penetrating through his left eye and the better portion of the back of his head blown off. Staff Sergeant Steele requested a status report from the squad leaders. They informed him that all Marines were accounted for. Aside from Second Squad, there were no additional casualties. All Marines were already "topped" off on ammo and ready for further attacks.

Returning to his squad, John and his teammates remained vigilant for the remainder of the night. It seemed like it had been forever since he had had a decent night's sleep. He was exhausted but ready for anything that might unexpectedly happen.

That evening John's platoon did not receive any further contact from the enemy. The silence was periodically broken as American jets flew over their fighting positions to strike their targets, muffling the whispers among the men. Each Marine was ready to prove his mettle in combat. In this silence John once again began to think about Susan and his family.

John had met Susan Williams in 2001, when he had taken a trip with one of his friends to visit the friend's family down in Alabama. As he walked the mall in downtown Huntsville with his friend, they strolled into a random jewelry store—the friend planned to propose to his girlfriend. Susan stood behind the counter and greeted them as they walked in.

"So, what are we shopping for today?" Susan said.

John's friend stated, "I'm looking for an engagement ring for my girlfriend."

"Well, we definitely have the perfect ring for your future fiancée," she responded.

As John's friend looked over the assortment of rings, John's attention was on Susan. She was exactly his type—brown hair and eyes, a little thicker (but he was OK with that). In his eyes, she was beautiful.

During the ensuing conversation, she found out John and his friend were Marines.

"Oh, I just love military guys; they are so hot," Susan exclaimed.

Susan looked at John and smiled. "So, do you have a girlfriend, John?" she said inquisitively.

John responded with a sly smile, "No, and I don't really have plans to have one either." John had already slept with several women, but his focus was on being a Marine, not relationships. As his friend purchased a ring, John and Susan traded phone numbers.

From the run-down Red Roof Inn in which he was staying, John called Susan and asked her, "So, when are you taking lunch?"

"In about twenty minutes," Susan responded.

"Well, you should come to my hotel for your lunch break."

"Sure, where are you staying?" she asked quizzically.

John gave her the address and his room number; within thirty minutes there was a knock on his door. John greeted Susan with a kiss, and after a little foreplay, John and Susan made the most of what time she had remaining in her lunch break.

Within three hours of meeting her, John had fucked Susan. A personal record for meeting and closing a sexual encounter for him at the time. Before he and his friend headed back to Camp Lejeune the next day, John and Susan met up a couple more times. They decided to see each other more, even though it was going to be a very long-distance relationship.

Over the next several months, John drove to Alabama as often as he could. On free weeknights they would talk on the phone for hours, getting to know each other better. This was John's first serious relationship, and he was happy that he had met such a great Christian woman— not really thinking negatively about how quickly he had been able to have sex with her.

He was very excited about what the future might hold and began to lose his love for the Marine Corps. John was increasingly putting Susan before the Marines and himself.

As time progressed John increasingly thought about proposing to Susan. He idealized her as a perfect woman to settle down and start a family with when he got out of the military. His future plans were changing to reflect her as a center point of his life.

Even during times when Susan would not answer the phone or claim she had plans with family on weekends he was off, John never thought anything of it. He trusted her and in his mind had no reason to doubt her or her loyalty.

As the sun began to rise over the Iraqi dessert, John snapped out of his daydream. The dead bodies remained strewn about the landscape. John refocused on his mission and ensured his men were awake and prepared for any orders coming down the chain. Shortly after, Staff

Sergeant Steele ordered John to take two fireteams (the equivalent of eight Marines) to conduct a quick recon of the area. His mission was to recover the three dead enemy soldiers and acquire any intel they could gather. The remaining dug-in Marines would provide cover for them should they receive contact.

John instructed each Marine on his duties. One team was going to establish a security perimeter around the dead as the other team did a quick recon around the immediate area. This being an open dessert, the men kept a low profile as they quickly made their way to their objective.

The area around the dead soldiers was strewn with empty brass shell casings, AK-47s lying in the dirt, and dried blood covering the sand. Once the area was secured and recon completed, John ordered one fireteam to remain as security. John and the recon team that had just returned searched the bodies for intel.

John began searching one of the corpses; he didn't find any intel, but what he found was incredibly valuable and definitely in short supply—cigarettes. Although the cigarettes were covered in mostly dry blood, this was a welcome sight for him. He had run out of smokes the day before; John was elated to get back to his lines and share a smoke with his men. He would have to air-dry away the blood, since cigarettes don't smoke well when wet.

John and his teammates returned to their lines and their positions after handing over the captured AKs and an empty rocket-propelled grenade (RPG) to the command. Now he was able to rest a little bit and smoke that much-needed cigarette. As he savored the first puff and the smoke filled his lungs, he became light headed.

The feeling was euphoric for him as he smoked and partook of his meal ready to eat (MRE). He was back again, alone with his thoughts. He thought of the young Marine that had died the night before. He had died so young and was only two years younger than John. It was only a matter of time before his family would be told the news of his death.

I am lucky, he thought to himself. At least he had had a chance to see some of the world before the world changed on 9/11. When he was in 1/8, as a young E-3, Lance Corporal Devereaux had been selected to join a Maritime Special Purpose Force (MSPF) platoon for an upcoming deployment to the Mediterranean under the 22nd Marine Expeditionary Unit (MEU) Special Operations Capable (SOC). The MSPF is a quick reactionary force that can be deployed anywhere within the region at a moment's notice, should an event or emergency arise.

There he trained alongside Force Reconnaissance Marines and received advanced infantry and special operations training. The training included Military Operations in Urban Terrain (MOUT), close quarters battle (CQB), ship search and seizure (a.k.a. visit, board, search and seizure [VBSS]), fast roping from helicopters, advanced medical field trauma training, and a host of other skills that would make him an even more effective killing instrument.

In November of 2001, John deployed with the 22nd MEU (SOC), living on the Navy's amphibious assault ship

USS *Nassau* (LHA-4) for six months before he met Susan. Because this was pre-9/11, the tenure was also known as a liberty cruise. There was no war zone to be deployed to, so the Marines conducted training with foreign militaries and had the opportunity to visit one liberty port after another.

John was finally able to see the world he had dreamed so much about. During his deployment, John had the opportunity to train with the Spanish Army, the Italian Army, Maltese Special Forces, the Tunisian Army, and the Croatian military.

Among the liberty ports John was able to experience were Rota and Cartagena in Spain, where he got his second arm tattoo in the back of a bar. In Italy he visited Rome, Naples, Brindisi, Taranto, and Vatican City, where he experienced authentic Italian food, Roman catacombs, old castles—one of which, according to legend, held the Holy Grail. He stood in Saint Peter's Square, known locally as Piazza San Pietro, where he heard and watched Pope John Paul II give a Christmas Eve benediction. He toured the port of Toulon in southern France, a small town in Croatia, and one of his favorite countries, Malta.

Returning to the United States after his six-month deployment, John had new ribbons on his chest and a new stripe added to his arm. Having been a Lance Corporal for just under a year and a half, he was now a Corporal (E-4) or NCO.

In the Marine Corps, the promotion to Corporal is a big milestone and a significant accomplishment in a junior enlisted Marine's career. The Marine Corps specializes in small-unit operations. Corporals hold a significant amount of authority and responsibility in commanding small contingents of Marines in combat and operations, including four-man fireteams.

John's promotion to Corporal consisted of two ceremonies. In the official ceremony, John's promotion warrant was read before the company, and he was pinned by the Company Commander and First Sergeant. The second, unspoken ceremony was conducted in private. This ceremony consisted of all the platoon's NCOs due to the sensitive fact that the nature of hazing had been highlighted throughout the Marine Corps.

The turtlebacks were removed from each of John's new Corporal insignias. Each NCO lined up to face John as he stood in the position of attention. Having ensured that the spikes on the back of the insignia were clear of the collar bone, each NCO punched and bottom-fisted the insignias on his collar, driving the spikes into his flesh, an act known as "pinning." Each subsequent punch drove the spikes deeper into the NCO's collar, causing the wound to bleed.

After every NCO had his turn punching the insignias into John's chest, it was time for him to earn his "blood stripes." Upon their promotion to Corporal, junior Marine NCOs receive a scarlet stripe on the outside seam of their uniform's trousers.

Although it has been proven historically inaccurate, legend holds that the red "blood stripe" worn on the trousers of officers and noncommissioned officers commemorates the nearly 90 percent casualty rate among

Marines who stormed the castle of Chapultepec during the Mexican-American War of 1847. The scarlet stripe seen today, with varying widths prescribed for different ranks, was officially adopted in 1904.

The platoon NCOs lined up in a two-column gauntlet (surprisingly known as "the gauntlet"). John would walk between the two columns, and an NCO on each side would knee him in the sides of his legs, giving each NCO a turn until John reached the end of the column. Barely able to stand up due to the excruciating pain, John had unofficially earned his blood stripes and was welcomed as a new member of the platoon NCO ranks.

There was a lot of divided thinking on whether these unofficial ceremonies were a form of hazing. John personally considered it an honor and a means of acceptance by the other NCOs. On rare occasions he'd seen some newly promoted NCOs not go through the initiation process; they were treated as outliers. They were outcasts within the NCO ranks and never really accepted or treated as NCOs.

As other Marines were welcomed home by their families, John looked around to see whether Susan or his family had come to welcome him home. It had been a week since he last talked to her on the phone, but he remembered her excitement at the prospect of seeing him and her promise that she would be there when he came back; John saw that she was not there and concluded she had never shown up.

He questioned why this was the case as he grabbed his gear and began the long walk back to his barracks.

After settling into his new room, he called Susan. Several rings on her phone. He hung up the phone and tried again. Still no response. He returned to his room, and his imagination turned to the many things that may have prevented her from being there or answering the phone.

It wasn't until a few days later that John received a call from Susan. She explained that she had lost her phone and that she didn't have the money to replace it—or to welcome him home from his first overseas tour. John was understanding and discussed plans to travel to Alabama that weekend to see her. John was always trying to find a way to get out of the barracks.

Marine barracks are a place where Marines typically drown their chronic depression with excessive alcoholism, cable TV, and video gaming. Since there's usually nothing to do in the barracks, unless you're hazing a boot Marine, a vehicle is essential for escaping to get more alcohol or go out in town to the local strip club, tattoo parlor, or Walmart. Most Marines without access to a vehicle remain in their barracks binge drinking their weekends away.

Some of the things John hated the most about barracks life were standing barracks duty (a period of twenty-four hours standing watch with little to no sleep); living with roommates; being surrounded by professional drunkards; Chinese field day every Thursday; and how typically everything was either broken, molded, or in total disrepair (and almost never fixed unless the Marine paid for it out of his pocket).

Centrally controlled AC blasted during the winter because it "saved money." When the AC was needed during the summer, it was usually broken. One other point John hated about barracks life: You couldn't escape the grasp of your command, since they knew where you lived. It was like they had this uncanny ability to know whether you were inside your room at any hour of the day.

Unlike married Marines, who lived in town, barracks Marines typically got chosen to do last-minute working parties, stand duty, or tend to a host of unforeseeable things that just happened on any typical Saturday morning. The key to living in the barracks for the weekend was to have plans and disappear on Friday night. If that was not possible, you had to ensure that your curtains were closed, that nobody could look into your room, and, under pain of death, that you never, ever answered your door when you heard a knock.

Thus John was always so eager to make plans for the weekends and go do things—he was still only eighteen years old and wasn't allowed to drink. Funnily enough, drinking overseas was acceptable, which may or may not have gotten him into a little bit of trouble, especially in light of beer being on tap at the local McDonald's in Spain.

John made plans to see Susan that weekend. Something seemed different with Susan. She really didn't ask many questions about John's deployment, nor did she go into too many details about what she had been up to while he had been away. John's stomach told him there was definitely something wrong. But he didn't know what.

John was less excited about seeing her than about finding out what was really going on. Why was she being so distant? Was it another man? Did she want to break up? John wanted the answer, no matter what it was. He could tell that there had been a change in her attitude because she interacted with him differently. This weekend he would find the answer.

Two days seemed to drag out as John waited for Friday to come, especially since he didn't talk to Susan during that time. When Friday came, John had already packed his luggage and filled his car up with gas. This way he could drive straight to Alabama after work to see her. So many thoughts continued to plague his mind during the eleven-hour trip from Camp Lejeune to Huntsville. He wasn't sure what was going to happen, but he had plenty of time to prepare for the worst.

John finally arrived in Huntsville around six in the morning. He called Susan to let her know he was in town. Since hotels weren't accepting guests until the afternoon, he stopped at a Waffle House for some breakfast and to gather his thoughts. He planned out what he was going to say to her, although he was internally unsure how either of them would react after not having seen each other and having had only intermittent phone contact for six months.

I should trust my instincts, he thought. Something was certainly off. Whatever it was, he wanted to know, so he could move on with his life, even if he had to hear the worst.

His phone rang as he ate breakfast; it was Susan.

"Hello," John replied.

"Hey, I'm not feeling very well this weekend. I'm sick in bed, and my body aches all over. Can we do another weekend?" Susan responded.

"But I'm already here in town, Susan. I drove eleven hours to get here to see you. What is going on with you? You seem different, and I want to know what's going on."

"John, I don't think it's a good idea for us to continue seeing each other."

"Why didn't you tell me this earlier, before I wasted my time and money driving down here to see you?" he asked angrily.

"Goodbye, John, and take care" was all he heard as she hung up the phone.

Frustrated and pissed, John finished his breakfast and decided to drive the eleven hours back to Camp Lejeune. *Fuck this shit*, he thought in his head. *I'm sure she was seeing another guy while I was gone on deployment.* He was unable to prove it. But he had suspected something was up, and her breaking up with him had proven that he should trust his gut instead of what she had told him.

Listening to oldies as he headed back to Camp Lejeune, he reasoned with himself about what had transpired. He concluded that she had found someone else who could be there for her and that his life didn't really matter that much. He considered himself expendable, so it was better off in the end that she found someone who would be there for her. What hurt him the most was how much attention he had paid to her instead of focusing on his mission and on being a stellar Marine.

CHAPTER 3

Barracks life returned to normal when he got back. John didn't think much about Susan after that. Occasionally he pondered what she was doing and whom she was doing it with. Thankfully his schedule was filled with additional training, so he didn't have too much time to dwell on her. Some nights he wanted to call her but actively resisted the temptation. On the flip slide of the coin, he knew that she probably wanted to call him too. She missed him (although a woman rarely ever tells her secrets).

Nearly six months went by with no contact, and out of the blue, John got a phone call. It was Susan.

"Hey, John, long time no talk. How have you been?"

"I've been good. Why are you calling me?"

"I regret breaking up with you the way I did, and I want to fix it. I miss you, John." It had been a long time since John had last spoken with her, and he had seen several other women; he thus felt indifferent about Susan and the breakup. He already assumed that whomever she left him for hadn't work out. Now she was trying to get back with him.

John really had no plans to reconnect with her. He would still fuck her, but it would be on his terms. He was no longer willing to drive eleven hours just for some pussy, especially since he was very busy training for another deployment to Okinawa. In a couple months he would be deploying with his new unit at Camp Lejeune, 3rd Battalion, 2nd Marines, Kilo Company, First Platoon, 2nd Marine Division (3/2).

"When can I see you?" Susan asked quizzically.

"I'm off this weekend, but you're going to have to come up here to see me."

"OK, I'll take Friday off from work and drive up. I'm excited to see you, babe!" Susan replied enthusiastically.

"All right. Sounds good. I'll see you Friday. You're paying for the hotel, since you can't stay in the barracks."

"That's fine, babe. I really want to see you."

As he hung up the phone, John thought about whether this was a good idea. *At least I will get some piece leaf this weekend*, he reasoned.

Friday evening arrived pretty quickly, since John was occupied with barracks room inspections, uniform and gear inspections, weapons cleaning, and working on his military studies for an upcoming meritorious promotion board to sergeant.

John's phone rang.

"Hey, babe. I just got to the base, and I'm getting a pass. Where can I meet you?" Susan asked.

"I'll meet you in front of the PX. I have my bag for the weekend, so we can just leave and get a hotel after you pick me up."

"Sounds good, babe. I'll see you soon!" Susan answered enthusiastically.

John wasn't sure what to expect as he waited for her to arrive. He knew that he should keep his feelings in check because of what she had done to him and not dredge up the past. His plan was to just have a good weekend, get some piece leaf, and enjoy his time away from the barracks.

John and Susan met in the PX (postal exchange) parking lot. Internally John was nervous, and he was pretty sure that Susan was too. As they greeted each other with hugs, John loaded his bags into her car, and they lightly chatted as they headed to the hotel to check in. Nothing of the past was brought up, as John was delighted to see her and was sure Susan felt the same way.

When they checked into their room, John and Susan embraced each other and began kissing, fondling, and crashing onto the bed. They spent the whole weekend fucking, dining out, relaxing, and just enjoying each other's company like old times. When it was time for Susan to leave, John thanked her for a great weekend, and she headed back down to Alabama.

As John continued to attend field op exercises for his upcoming deployment to Japan, he continued to talk with Susan on a regular basis. She would try to come to Camp Lejeune at least once a month to see John and rekindle what they'd had in the past. Because he wasn't in a relationship with her, he still regularly slept with other women and primarily thought of Susan as a friend with benefits.

He was damn sure he wasn't going to make the same mistake he had with Susan by getting into a new relationship or developing an emotional attachment to a woman before another six-month-long deployment. He had learned his lesson the first time around, or so he thought.

After being in the Marine Corps for a couple years, John had seen and experienced firsthand what happened to married and long-term-relationship (LTR) Marines when they deployed. It was often the case that when a unit deployed to wherever in the world, that same night all of the military spouses and girlfriends/boyfriends would fill up the clubs looking for fun.

Without fail. Every. Single. Time. Some spouses were discreet about it; others blatantly left their rings on their fingers as they cheated. John had slept with several married women. Not something to be proud of, but for him it was just about sex, and that was it—nothing that would involve emotions or a relationship.

Marines would find out while deployed, either through a Dear John letter or via friends back home catching their spouses doing things they were not supposed to be doing, that their significant others were being unfaithful. Some broke down and cried, others got very pissed, while still others accepted this as a part of being in the military.

The ones who accepted this behavior—it was usually just a kink, or they were afraid to lose the "one" and willing to do anything to keep the "one" happy so they would not leave them. Some of the spouses would even go into the barracks stateside and have a train of young Marines run on them. There was no shame in it at all.

In one instance John witnessed a woman get passed around from one platoon to the next, from one floor to the next. She must have had fifty guys in that one night. The reason why John knew it was about fifty guys was because they all eventually contracted an STD from her and had to go to medical later in the week and get medicine to kill whatever STD they had.

Seeing that the majority of married Marines ended up divorced astounded John. He questioned why any Marine in his right mind would want to get married while in the military, only to get divorce raped or have false allegations placed on him. This would certainly ruin the Marine's future career in the military; he would lose his kids and sometimes half his retirement pension (usually after ten years of marriage within the service the spouse is entitled to half of a Marine pension). Not to mention that he would have to pay alimony and child support without ever really seeing his kids again. This is one of the main reasons why John reasoned that he would not get married while in the military.

On September 11, 2001, John was teaching a marksmanship course in anticipation of his unit going to the range the next week. As he was giving his period of instruction, someone burst into the classroom and turned on the two TVs. One of the World Trade Center towers had been struck by an aircraft.

The Marines sat silently as they watched the tower burning and people jumping to their deaths. Some questioned whether it was a mistake; some commented that it was a terrorist attack. But that moment in time seemed to freeze. Each Marine waiting for an update while some who had family in New York City tried to contact their relatives to see if they were OK.

Suddenly another plane struck the second tower. A loud "ooh" was belted out by the Marines. "We're at war!" some commented. This was definitely not an accident. That plane had intentionally flown into the second tower. Many of the Marines realized in that moment America was now at war—with whom was to be determined, but everything would change from that point on.

The battalion commander ordered an emergency formation, and the entire battalion area was locked down and secured. Armed duty was instructed to conduct guard and roving patrols of the battalion area. All liberty was suspended with the exception of married Marines, who were allowed to return to their homes but had to remain in on-call status.

Security was increased all over the base, and all Marines were advised to ensure their military IDs were on them at all times. This heightened threat level didn't stop operations and training. Now more than ever, the Marines of 3/2 knew how vitally important next week's rifle range was going to be.

A couple months after 9/11, 3/2 deployed to Marine Corps Base Camp Schwab in Okinawa for its routine six-month deployment. The base had a great beach, and the snorkeling was some of the best in the world. Most of the Okinawan people were kind, quiet, and respectful to the Americans on the island.

Living in the barracks on Camp Schwab was similar to living in the barracks at Camp Lejeune back home. Mostly the same things you would find on any regular base—a PX, chow hall, and rec center. There is a saying that in Okinawa you either become a professional drinker or you become devoutly religious. Apparently there is no in-between.

On deployment John would conduct jungle training at the Jungle Warfare Training Center (JWTC) during the week and make use of his weekends to explore the whole island. There was lots to see and do; he also happened to catch the eye of a Japanese woman in her midthirties named Yoko Watanabe, who worked at the base PX.

She was short and very beautiful but also happened to be a single mother to a young boy no older than two years old. Although John still occasionally talked with Susan back home, he and Yoko would spend their weekends together, and she would explore the island with him. They knew nothing serious was going to develop between them, since he was only going to be on the island for a few months. So they kept it casual as friends with benefits.

Halfway through his deployment, John and his company were sent to the mainland of Japan, to a place near Mount Fuji, to conduct cold-weather training with the Japanese Army. This was the first time John had to learn how to ski with full military gear on and with a sled towed behind him. The primary thing that John learned about the Marines was that they could take anything potentially fun and make it just completely suck.

The Japanese Army was very efficient in how it conducted cold-weather training. As the Marines dug fighting positions, the Japanese built a complete underground tunnel system in the snow in the same amount of time. Training with the Japanese soldiers was a lot of fun for John, and he learned a great deal about their culture. The Marines and soldiers would drink sake out of wooden boxes, shouting "*kampai!*" until the late hours of the evening, only to be woken up for early morning physical training. The Japanese soldiers could drink just as much as, if not more than, John and the other Marines.

One interesting thing John experienced during his time training with the Japanese Army was how they bathed. In the barracks each soldier would sit on his bucket. They would soap up and wash their bodies, and while naked they would go to a couple hot tub–sized pools with about ten other naked men in each pool. There was definitely no modesty, since there were nearly fifty men in one room, sitting in pools, naked as the day there were born, just chatting about random bullshit like people would do on a smoke break.

Before the cold-weather training came to an end, John had the opportunity to visit Tokyo, which was one of the biggest cities he had ever seen at that point in his life. It seemed even bigger than New York. The buildings were tall, there were lights and signs everywhere, and the streets and subways were overcrowded with people.

John was delighted to experience the Japanese culture and enjoy the Japanese food—well, some of it, at least.

Some of it was very weird but also very delicious; however, everything was very expensive. John and several of his friends started to barhop within the Roppongi district. Several bars later one of his friends who was severely drunk threw up all over John and the table they were sitting at. After having been kicked out of the bar, the group returned to their rooms to sleep off their drunkenness, though not before some of the guys pissed on parked cars on the street along the way.

Just before leaving Camp Fuji, John was meritoriously promoted to Sergeant (E-5). He had done what few Marines could do within their first enlistment—made the rank of Sergeant. John's career in the Marines was certainly on the fast track. He was well respected within the platoon and the company. He was liked by everyone and considered a natural leader and an outstanding model Marine by the command.

Now having added a third stripe to his uniform, John didn't have to go through the NCO hazing process as he did as a Corporal. Typically a newly promoted Sergeant would get together with the other Sergeants in the platoon and take the pay difference between Corporal and Sergeant to buy booze and get shitfaced. Because he was still on Camp Fuji, that unofficial ceremony would have to wait until he got back to Okinawa in a few days.

Upon returning to Camp Schwab in Okinawa, John settled into his new barracks room, reconnected with Yoko, called his family, and talked with Susan. With only two months left before they returned home, a lot of the Marines were eager to get back to the States. One Saturday night John heard a couple Marines arguing in their room next door. He knocked on the door to find out what was going on.

One of the Marines, Lance Corporal Evans, had just returned from a night on the town and was very intoxicated and aggressive. He had found out through a friend back home that his girlfriend had had a small gangbang with three Marines and that she was leaving him. You could tell he was hurt and angry, unable to emotionally process what had happened. John tried to calm him down and advised him to sleep it off.

Evans took a swing at John; John evaded the punch and counteracted with a right hook that landed on Evans's left eyebrow, opening the skin. Blood started spurting out of the wound, and several Marines held Evans down as they tried to contain the bleeding. The platoon doc came into the room and told John that Evans had to be taken to the Basic Aid Station (BAS) to have his wound stitched up.

John advised the doc that he would help take Evans to BAS because Evans was too drunk to walk on his own. As they walked to BAS, Evans fell down a small flight of stairs and nearly broke his ankle. He was a total mess, but the alcohol numbed the pain.

"Surely he will feel this in the morning," the doc said.

John only responding with "Yeah, he will."

After Evans was treated, he was escorted back to the barracks room to sleep off his drunkenness. John instructed the platoon to assemble in the common area so he could talk with them.

"I'm sure you're aware of what happened tonight. He's drunk and fucked up," John began. "Whatever happened tonight will remain with us, and we will not talk about it further. I'm not doing any paperwork on him; he's in a bad place right now, and paperwork won't solve the problem. He tripped and fell down a flight of stairs tonight, and that will be the end of it. The platoon sergeant and lieutenant have already been advised of what happened, and, like I said, we're not going to bring it up again."

As he looked at Evans's roommates, he commanded, "Make sure you keep an eye on him, and make sure he doesn't do anything stupid. If you have any issues, come to me, and I'll take care of it."

The platoon was dismissed, and everyone returned to their rooms for the remainder of the evening. About a week later, John was returning to the barracks after leaving the company office when he heard a lot of commotion. As he entered the barracks, there were several Marines standing outside of Lance Corporal Evans's door.

John walked into the room and was not prepared for what he saw. Evans had fashioned a noose out of 550 cord and had hanged himself in the room; a note on his bed detailed how life had not been worth living since he had lost his girlfriend. He hadn't seen a future and had not been able live anymore without her.

The room was secured; all the Marines were taken out of the room as John and Evans's team leader, Corporal Meady, remained. The base police were contacted, and the chain of command was immediately notified. After John and other members of the platoon gave their statements, John returned to his room.

He began thinking about the fact that he had almost killed himself when he was thirteen. He could somewhat relate to Evans being in that dark place because he had been there as well at one point in his life.

No woman is worth killing yourself over, he reasoned in his head.

But there was nothing he could do at that point besides make sure his Marines were OK and that they could talk to him if they needed to.

The remainder of his time on Okinawa was mostly uneventful. Days were filled with physical training (PT), snorkeling, and relaxing when he could. He was ready to get back to the States. The relationship between John and Yoko ended when he found out she was seeing a few other Marines as well. John was definitely not her first and certainly was not going to be her last.

She just wants to get pregnant, trap a Marine, and get married so she can come to the land of the big PX. He laughed to himself.

John hadn't developed an emotional attachment to Yoko, so her absence didn't really matter all that much. He was fairly indifferent about it all actually. *All things come to an end,* he reasoned. He was about to leave the island soon anyway, and he wasn't really surprised Yoko would attach herself to another guy—or guys—before he left. He certainly wasn't going to take her back to the

States with him. Besides, he still had Susan and a couple other women he was talking to and fucking on the side.

Upon returning to the States, with two deployments under his belt and more ribbons added to his chest, he was hopeful he would have a chance to go to Afghanistan and fight the Taliban. However, since John was a primary marksmanship instructor and an expert in the rifle and pistol, he was nominated to be a range coach at the rifle range in Stone Bay, a satellite base near Camp Lejeune. It was going to be a temporary additional duty (TAD) assignment lasting for only six months.

Having moved into yet another barracks, John had his own room for the first time. It was quiet, with no neighbors, and so many of the rules were relaxed. He didn't have to Chinese field day his room anymore, just make sure it was clean. He had his own chair and TV; he could watch whatever he wanted. The biggest bonus was that he could come and go as he pleased. It was absolutely great. He even had multiple women come over without any problems or unnecessary attention. John felt spoiled and dreaded his TAD ending.

Susan continued to drive up from Alabama to visit John and increasingly talked about getting back into a relationship. John could sense this desire in her but didn't want to restart a relationship that had failed in the past. A few weeks after seeing Susan, John got a voice mail from her.

"John, please call me when you get this; we need to talk," she stated.

Whenever someone says, "We need to talk," you know you're about to receive some bad news. When he got off work, he called her back.

"Hey, I got your voice mail; what's going on? What do we need to talk about?"

"John, I'm pregnant," she quietly stated.

"You're pregnant? Is it mine?" he questioned.

"Yes, John, I've only been with you. I love you, John. What are we going to do?"

John's mind was filled with so many thoughts. Was she telling the truth? Was it his? What was he going to do now? Should he "do the right thing" and marry her? John felt his life was going to be changed forever. He felt stuck in a situation that he could not get out of because he and Susan didn't believe in abortion.

John accepted the fact that he was going to be a dad, like it or not, and that scared the shit out of him. John had seen how divorce in the military was all too common. He was only twenty years old, and now he was going to be a father. Over the phone John proposed to Susan and said they were going to get married. Susan was ecstatic to hear his response and said she couldn't wait to see him again.

Approximately a week later, John received orders to return to his previous unit, 3/2, a full month early. When John returned to his unit, scuttlebutt (the rumor mill) claimed that the unit was about to deploy to the Middle East sometime in January, which was only a month away. Tensions between the United States and Iraq were escalating.

There was very little time to prepare for such a last-minute deployment. However, since the Marine Corps prides itself on being in a constant state of readiness, all of the preparations were made quickly. Two weeks of leave were granted to everyone for Christmas because nobody knew how long this deployment was going to be.

Instead of visiting Susan for his leave period, John returned home for the first time in a long time to see his family. His family could barely recognize him when he arrived and noticed how much John had changed as a man. John was not surprised to see how Robert continued to drink heavily, having gained over thirty pounds since John last saw him.

They greeted each other with a firm handshake, and he gave his mother a hug. He noticed she no longer had any teeth in her mouth and had noticeably aged since he last saw her. *Robert and Linda certainly are not aging well,* he thought. Savanah was in college by this time, and his stepsister Julie had grown up considerably from the last time he had seen her.

While he was home, John visited his family and some friends, although he remained detached from everyone. All could see the change in him and his transformation since school. John was living life on his terms, a stark contrast to what he had experienced growing up.

Even the girls who had gone to school with John saw him differently. They frequently gave him their phone numbers. Having not forgotten how he was treated in school and noting that a majority of these girls had gained so much weight or were already single mothers, he politely accepted their phone numbers but had no intention of ever contacting them.

CHAPTER 4

On New Year's Eve of 2003, John received a call from his command and was ordered back to base immediately. All leave was canceled, and the battalion was recalling everyone. There just so happened to be a big snowstorm in the area. After John packed his bags, he began heading back to base on the ice-covered roads.

As he was driving, his car hit a patch of ice. He skidded off the road and struck a guard rail on the rear passenger side of the vehicle. The New York State Police arrived shortly thereafter, along with a tow truck to pull John's vehicle out of the ditch. With his car still drivable, John decided to push on to the next town, Saratoga Springs, and spend the night while the storm passed through.

Leaving early next morning, John restarted his trek back to Camp Lejeune. The weather had dramatically improved from the day before, and John was thankful there were no further incidents. Returning to his unit, John was advised they were about to get a "boot drop," a reinforcement of Marines just out of the School of Infantry (SOI), within the next couple days.

John remembered when he joined 1/8 after graduating SOI. He and the other platoon NCOs were going to make sure these new Marines were squared away for the upcoming deployment. The unit was leaving within the next couple days to head to Naval Station Norfolk. There was no time to mess around or play any "boot" games like the ones he had experienced. Shit was real, and John had to make sure his new Marines were ready to go.

Scuttlebutt rumored they were going to head to Kuwait in preparation for a war with Iraq. There were mixed emotions among the Marines, especially the boots. Some were fearlessly brave, others outwardly projected confidence and bravado but internally were scared shitless, and a select few made their cowardice known.

One boot Marine just out of SOI jumped off the third story balcony and broke his leg; several others also deserted the unit. Some Marines caused serious injury to themselves so they wouldn't have to deploy. In those moments before the deployment, you could really see what every Marine was made of—at least at face value.

John, who did not give a shit about his life and whether he lived or died, was excited. He thought about Susan and his unborn baby; he pondered how they would do should anything happen to him. In all reality it didn't matter, because he was going to go regardless of the possible outcome.

Before he prepared to leave, John called Susan to say that he was shipping out the next day and that he would be fine. Crying on the phone, Susan was very upset that she wasn't going to be able to see John before he left.

Comforting her, he told her that everything was going to be all right and that he would be back in no time. He told her he hoped he would be there for the birth of his baby but couldn't make any promises.

Pre-invasion Deployment from Camp Lejeune

Approximately seventy-one hundred Marines and sailors departed Marine Corps Base Camp Lejeune, North Carolina, on January 15, 2003. Transported by bus to Naval Station Norfolk in Virginia, the Marines and sailors were divided among seven US Navy ships: USS *Kearsarge* (LHD-3), USS *Saipan* (LHA-2), USS *Bataan* (LHD-5), USS *Ashland* (LSD-48), USS *Portland* (LSD-37), USS *Gunston Hall* (LSD-44), and USS *Ponce* (LPD-15). John's unit was assigned to the USS *Kearsarge*.

Ship life was as John had remembered it from his first deployment in the Mediterranean. This time was different, though—he was heading to Kuwait to prestage for a possible invasion of Iraq. There were definitely not going to be any liberty port visits this time around. John knew he was probably heading to war, something he had wanted to do when he was a young child. Maybe his prophecy of dying in combat was about to be a reality, so he took the time to prepare himself mentally and physically for whatever might happen.

John pondered, *If I get killed, how will it happen? Will I be alive one minute, and then will there be total darkness the next? Is it going to be painful? Or will I get wounded and return home, prophecy unfulfilled?* So many unanswered questions, but he accepted his fate.

For a month John and his Marines conducted training every day on ship. He made sure the Marines were ready for what they were about to face. Having passed through the Strait of Gibraltar, through the Mediterranean Sea and the Suez Canal into the Red Sea, they would be at their destination soon enough.

During this time, John called his family and Susan every chance he got. One day on the smoke deck, while talking with one of his friends, a cute blond sailor asked to borrow a lighter from John. John handed her his lighter and said, "Hi, I'm John."

"I'm Amber," she replied. John was immediately attracted to her, and he could tell she was attracted to him as well.

The small talk lasted a couple cigarettes. Having learned she worked on the ship's diesel engines, John was now anticipating getting some chow for the evening. Amber asked if she could join him and his friends.

"Sure, come along," John replied.

As they all sat down at dinner, Amber sat next to John, and they continued to talk about their homes and where they were from back in the States. This encounter seeming to be more than just a dinner in the mess hall. By all appearances it seemed to be a first date, just located on a Navy amphibious warship heading to war.

After dinner John and Amber went back to the smoke deck to have one final cigarette before he hit the rack. Standing in a dark corner on the smoke deck with the night sky above them, ensuring nobody was paying attention, Amber touched John's hand in a seductive way and smiled. John took the hint, smiled, and winked back, showing his acceptance of her advances.

"Do you want to come down to see my shop after this smoke?" she asked.

"Sure, that would be great," he replied as they finished their cigarettes; she escorted him down to her shop, where they were all alone.

As Amber showed him around the shop, they went to a back room. Having ensured that they were alone, Amber walked up to John and began kissing him passionately. Touching and exploring each other's bodies, they slowly began to undress each other. Since the door couldn't be locked, John and Susan knew they had to be quick. John unzipped Amber's Navy coveralls and pulled them down as Amber undid the buttons of John's camouflage blouse and removed it.

He exposed her breasts and began to suck her pink nipples. Amber arched her head back, enjoying the sensation of his tongue. John fucked Amber for several minutes before finishing quickly to avoid getting caught. The room smelled like sex as they quickly put their uniforms back on.

"That was great; let's go grab a smoke before I hit the rack," John said to Amber.

"That felt amazing," Amber responded as they exited her shop.

As they walked up the long ladder well to the smoke deck, Amber passed one of her coworkers heading down to the shop they had just had sex in. Surely he would know what just happened in there, but he was very laid back and wouldn't care.

John and Amber would continue seeing each other on the smoke deck, eating chow, and having sex whenever they had the chance. They almost got caught a couple times, but thankfully they didn't, because that would have put John and Amber in some serious trouble. Sex on the ship was not tolerated.

At one point two male Marines, not in John's platoon, were caught having sex on the back of the ship. Both of them were punished and removed from the ship. Their military careers were over because homosexuality at that time was under a different policy and not tolerated, and nor was violating an article under the Uniform Code of Military Justice (UCMJ).

The day before debarking from the *Kearsarge*, John called his family and Susan to tell them that he was OK and that he would see them soon. John asked Susan about the baby and her only response was "I'm OK; everything is fine." John once again thought in his gut that there was something wrong. What it was, he had no idea; he just knew something seemed off with her once again.

After talking to Susan, John met up with Amber. Amber was emotionally attached to John and cried at the thought of him leaving and heading into a war where he could get killed.

Amber promised John she would write him and send him packages with cigarettes in them every chance she got. John smiled at Amber and comforted her by saying,

"Don't worry about anything; I will be fine. Nothing will happen, and I'll be back sooner than you realize."

Realistically speaking, John had no idea what was going to happen or if he would be back at all. His fate was unknown. That was a big part of the reason John had decided to have sex with Amber in the first place. If he was going to war with the possibility of not coming back, he was going to have some fun while he still could. No guilt. No remorse. His conscience was clear.

The day finally came. On February 15 John's unit was ordered to debark from the ship and helicoptered into the northern Kuwaiti desert. Before they were transported off the ship, all of their gear was prestaged in the hangar bay. John received over one thousand rounds of 5.56 ammunition, a bandolier of 40 mm grenades for his M-203 grenade launcher, a couple hand grenades—all his magazines were loaded to the max. *This is really happening*, he thought to himself as he ensured his Marines had their ammunition and equipment ready to go.

The amount of gear John and his Marines had to carry was mindboggling—rifle, ammunition, body armor, helmets, and NBC MOPP (nuclear, biological, or chemical mission-oriented protective posture) suits to protect against chemical warfare. Their packs were filled with clothing, gear, trenching shovels, and sleeping bags. The list continued on, and the equipment totaled over one hundred pounds. It took two Marines to lift one Marine off the ground their equipment was so heavy.

STAGING IN KUWAIT

Climbing up the steep ramps heading to the flight deck, John smiled to Amber as he walked by. Tears filled her eyes as she worried what would happen to him. They loaded the CH-46 helicopter, tightly packed with all of their gear, weapon muzzles facing the floor; John was on his way to Kuwait.

The helicopter ride lasted about thirty minutes. As they debarked the helicopter, the impact of the heat was immediate. They had to march just under a mile to their destination, Camp Shoup, which would have been a difficult task in any terrain, but especially in the brutal desert heat and sand.

Life in Camp Shoup had none of the luxuries of a conventional base like Camp Lejeune. It was a village of canvas tents neatly organized and built by the advanced working party; high walls of sand surrounded the compound. Seventeen to twenty men slept on the ground in each tent, with no electricity, no running water; for security reasons, no lights were allowed on after dark.

There were no buildings; there was no PX from which to buy something. Supplies brought to the camp arrived in packages or from the ships anchored offshore. Essential items were rationed, since they had no clue when or where they would be able to replenish their cigarettes, chewing tobacco, and other items.

In addition John and his men would stand in long lines for mediocre food and were only allowed to shower once every four days. Living in such tight quarters at all times, everyone got used to the pungent smell of the other

Marines. Despite training eight to ten hours every day and profusely sweating in the desert heat, John became accustomed to showering every four days.

Each Marine had two sets of desert camouflage uniforms but had no ability to wash them. They were instructed to wear only one uniform in Kuwait. If there was an invasion into Iraq, they could change into the second, "clean" one. The sense of being refreshed John felt when he did get his shower every fourth day was quickly forgotten when he had to put back on his sweat-drenched uniform and gear. John and his Marines also had to shave their heads because a thick layer of sand would cake on their scalps. Certainly, a hot fucking mess.

Gas masks were an essential part of the gear, as they had to be within reach in the event of an NBC attack. John and his men trained to effectively don (put on, clear, and ensure a proper seal on) their gas masks within seconds.

A Marine has about nine seconds to put on a gas mask—that's the difference between life and death in a chemical or biological attack. Additionally John continued training, simulating combat operations in an NBC environment, and practicing decontamination techniques. The NBC threat was very real, since the premise of the now seemingly imminent invasion was to find chemical weapons in Iraq.

It was also known based on history that Iraq's dictator, Saddam Hussein, had the potential to unleash chemical attacks on the Marines. This had been proven during the Iran-Iraq War of 1980 to 1988, during which Hussein had used chemical attacks on Iranian military forces and civilian populations, costing the lives of tens of thousands of people.

For just over a month, the Marines trained and prepared for any attack Saddam and the Iraqi Army might unleash. John realized he was going to go home through Iraq or death. There was no way the US government was going to spend billions of dollars staging its forces all over Kuwait if there wasn't going to be an invasion.

Internally John knew they were going to invade Iraq. It was just a matter of time. Other Marines quietly talked about rumors that they were going to be heading home soon. John laughed at the hilarious optimism.

Despite the hardships John and his men faced, their spirits remained high. Once training was finished for the day and night came, the laughter and voices of the men drifted out of the tents. To entertain themselves and pass the time, they played card games (especially spades, which John absolutely wanted no part of), good-naturedly insulted each other, and exchanged pictures of girlfriends, wives, and family. John, however, never talked about home or his family or really shared anything personal with anyone. He wanted his past to remain his past. He had a new life within the Marine Corps, and there was no need for anyone to know more than that.

Away from their families, sometimes for the first time ever, the Marines found entertainment among themselves. Impromptu touch football games were organized, and regular wrestling matches called "bull in the ring" honed their fighting ability. Fun physical training used as a way to keep the men mentally and physically sharp.

Even facing imminent war, the Marines were more concerned over the rumors that the singer and actress Jennifer Lopez had been killed in a car crash. Frustration eventually began stirring in the camp because they knew they were there to do their part, to do their job to the best of their ability or die trying.

Mail started to trickle in slowly as John received several letters from his family, Susan, and Amber. Mostly they talked about how they were proud of John and that they hoped he was safe. They would share news from back home and express that things were not looking very good on the war-political front.

Because there was no source of outside information, John had no idea what was happening in the real world. The only information the men received was via these outside letters. Sometimes his letters contained pictures so John could keep them on his person to remind him of home.

Surprisingly, Amber was writing to John more than Susan was. He had only received one letter from Susan, and it did not discuss the baby. John had a feeling Susan probably wasn't pregnant. After all, he hadn't seen or had sex with her since the end of October. Surely at five months, she would be sharing sonogram images or pictures of her belly growing. It all seemed suspicious to him.

She probably claimed to be pregnant to get me to marry her, and since we haven't had sex, she lost her opportunity to get pregnant for real, he reasoned. Whatever it was, he was going to trust his gut and just let things unfold when he got back to the States, *if* he got back to the States.

John and his men were not told when or where they would go, although they pretty much had an idea that they were going to get their first taste of combat when they invaded Iraq. What they did know was that they were ready, and the sobering reality was that some men would make it and others would pay the full price for their country.

When a person signs up for the military, regardless of branch, they write a blank check to the US government up to and including life for their country. It's a sobering reality for many to know that they may not live long enough to see their families again.

In the first week of March, the commander held a formation of the company. He addressed his Marines, advising them to make sure any final letters to be mailed were sent within the next couple days. The camp was no longer going to be receiving or sending out mail. Everyone had already completed last wills and powers of attorney. John had previously signed a waiver since he was the last living male in his family who could carry on the family name. If John died, that would be an end to the Deveraux line.

The commander's final statement to his men was "Make sure you have your blood type on your boots, helmets, and sleeves. Keep your dog tags on you at all times because that might be the only way we can identify your body."

The Marines suspected something was about to happen and that the invasion was imminent due to the mail stoppage. The mail was their only means of contact with the outside world. This was going to be their first taste of combat, and every Marine there was ready to do their job instead of training. John and his men had taken down family names and addresses with promises to talk to parents in the event any of them were killed. Everyone was as prepared as he could be. Whatever was going to happen, they were eager and ready.

On March 18 each Marine was allowed to call home for two minutes on a satellite phone. As John called his family, he told them he loved them and that he was OK. His mother was crying on the other end, happy to hear his voice.

"Be careful wherever you are, because the news looks really bad," she stated.

Little did she know this was possibly the last time she would ever hear her son's voice. As he said his goodbyes to her and the rest of his family, he walked back to his tent, unsure of what he felt about all of it. Mostly the feeling of surrealness.

On March 19, 2003, the Marines loaded onto five-ton trucks with full MOPP gear on. With clean weapons and loaded down with the ammunition they had received from the *Kearsarge*, they began the invasion of Iraq. In the desert heat, wearing a MOPP suit was like wearing winter pants and a winter jacket in 105-degree heat. It's something you really have to experience to appreciate how much it sucks.

Crossing the line of departure (LOD) the Marines were told "*Gas! Gas! Gas!*" as they crossed the border into Iraq. Each Marine was frantic to get his gas mask on within the nine-second time frame. For the first time, they felt the reality of fear and death.

Thankfully the gas attack was not a real attack, but the ever-present danger remained a reality. As the long convoy of trucks loaded down with Marines stopped, one Marine jumped off a truck and stripped off all his gear; explosive diarrhea shot out of his ass onto the desert floor in front of a battalion of hundreds of Marines, all of them cheering and telling him to give it hell. There is no shame or modesty among the Marines; you do what you have to do. The invasion of Iraq had just begun.

CHAPTER 5

John woke up with his M-203 rifle pointed to his face and the selector on fire. Had he accidentally pulled the trigger, he would have shot himself in the head. The M-203 is a single-shot, 40 mm under barrel grenade launcher attached under an M-16 or variant rifle. Delusional due to the severe sleep deprivation he was experiencing, he quickly made his weapon safe but didn't realize where he was for a few moments.

Surrounded by the sand they had dug into the night before, he made sure the welfare of his men was taken care of. They all had chow and were loaded up with ammo. As John began to drift back to his thoughts, his platoon received orders to pack up their gear and get ready for another movement. Destination unknown—but they were heading deeper into Iraq. After they loaded into the trucks, they headed north along Highway 1.

The weather was excruciatingly hot as the men— loaded down with MOPP gear, combat gear, and ammunition—sat in the backs of the trucks with the sun directly beating on them, all the while trying to maintain vigilance. Some of the men would rotate shifts of sleeping and providing security. About thirty minutes into their trip north, the convoy veered off the highway, and the Marines were ordered to set up fighting positions. Just as the fighting positions were finished, orders were to once again head north. So the men loaded back into the trucks, the fighting positions they made were filled back in, and once again they began heading north.

A lot of the countryside looked like barren desert; a large interstate highway with traffic signs written in Arabic cut the landscape in half. The men had been awake for over ninety hours. They were physically and mentally drained; some had severe cases of diarrhea. At one stop several Marines jumped off the truck and immediately stripped out of their MOPP gear in hurried attempts not to shit their pants. Just as they had done at the beginning of the invasion, the other Marines in the trucks cheered.

COMBAT OPERATIONS BEGIN

The convoy had been continuing north for about an hour when several vehicles in the convoy started to receive small-arms fire. Amid the confusion nobody in John's truck knew where it was coming from. John ordered them to get off their truck and provide 180-degree security until they could determine the direction of the shots being fired.

As the men scanned the surrounding area, John saw one Marine a couple vehicles ahead take a round in the chest and watched as his lifeless body fell to the ground.

Two Marines next to the fallen Marine were covered in his blood, unsure if they had been shot as well. Making sure his men weren't wounded, John continued to scan the area as he remained with his Marines. He noticed the convoy was taking fire from both sides as he heard bullets impacting their truck.

Using the dirt and rocky terrain, the dug-in enemy forces utilized natural cover and concealment to ambush the convoy. The lead truck in the convoy remained untouched as RPGs impacted the second and third trucks, with additional RPGs impacting a couple of the last trucks in the convoy in a well-coordinated attack.

As the ambush intensified, the enemy took out the lead and follow vehicles, cutting off any possibility of escape. Once the trucks were damaged, the enemy focused its attack on the center of the convoy, also known as the "killing zone." The goal was to fill the killing zone with a lot of destruction and a lot of dead American bodies.

The Marines began to return fire at the enemy positions after the initial confusion was over. Lieutenant Smith called in air support as bullets impacted the truck around him. Within minutes AH-1 Cobra attack helicopters arrived and began suppressing the enemy fire on both sides of the convoy with machine gun fire and precision rocket strikes.

For what seemed like several minutes, gunfire from the enemy positions ceased. John instructed his men to put in fresh mags and keep alert. He overheard on the radio that his company was going to secure the right flank of the convoy. Another company, Lima Company, was ordered to secure the left flank.

John told his men, "We're about to check and secure the area in front of us. Lima Company is going to check the other side. Keep your spacing and stay alert."

"Roger that, Sergeant!" his men replied.

So far John hadn't lost a man on his team, and he wasn't about to have that happen now. A few moments later, both companies began patrolling outward, ever alert for further enemy contact. The Marines walked a couple hundred yards until they reached the enemy fighting positions, unsure of what to expect or what they would encounter.

Up to this point, they hadn't had any further enemy contact since the initial ambush. As the Marines reached the enemy positions, they understood why. John was unsure of how many enemy combatants lay dead before him as he gazed upon strewn body parts. One combatant who stood out didn't have a face; he was missing an arm, and his body was mutilated beyond recognition.

John had seen some gruesome things, but had never experienced carnage of such magnitude. Pieces of human flesh, intestines, bone mater, limbs, fingers strewn about in a sand-dried sea of blood. A couple of the Marines threw up at the sight before them, having never been personally exposed to such gore, while other Marines said, "Fuck yeah, get some!"

John held a quiet reserve as he instructed his Marines to gather the weapons and any intel they could find on the bodies, despite the Iraqis' status as enemy combatants who had certainly tried to kill him and his men.

"Sergeant, there is not really anything left of these fuckers to check," one of his men said.

"Just do what the fuck I told you and check the god-damn bodies so we can get the fuck out of here," John retorted.

Another Marine asked John, "What are we going to do with the bodies—well, what's left of them—Sergeant?"

"Nothing. We're going to leave them here," he responded.

After they left the bodies and returned to the convoy, the battalion commander wanted a damage assessment completed. Six trucks had been damaged or destroyed; several of them only had bullet impacts but were still functionally operational. Three Marines had been killed and another eleven wounded. John was thankful that none of his men had been killed or wounded, but he did lose a good friend whom he went to boot camp with.

The convoy received orders to rescue the remnants of a US Army convoy from the 507th Maintenance Company. The convoy had mistakenly veered off Highway 8 onto Highway 7 and was under attack near An Nasiriyah, a city still considered enemy-held territory. Although there was very little information, apparently the Army convoy was being ambushed just as John's unit had been earlier. Several soldiers were reported killed, and several more had been taken prisoner as they tried to escape the city.

As John's convoy arrived at the outskirts of An Nasiriyah around sunset, he saw at least fifteen destroyed vehicles as they began to receive sporadic small-arms fire, the source and direction of which were unknown. As John and his Marines set up defensive positions away from the trucks, there was in increase in small-arms fire. Suddenly explosions erupted from RPG, mortar rounds, and tank gunfire a couple hundred yards in front of them. There was no time to be afraid. Their training kicked in, and they began to return fire and call in air and artillery strikes.

There was no time to think about home, family, or loved ones. Right now, the only concern facing John and the Marines was killing the enemy Iraqi soldiers and not getting killed themselves. The firefight ended as quickly as it had started once nightfall came. Thankfully, there were no casualties in his unit, and John was ordered to have his men dig in defensive positions. Tomorrow they were going to take the city. After all the positions were made, a van without lights began to approach their position.

The Marines lit the truck up with small-arms fire, and it stopped dead in its tracks. Through NVGs they could see several armed men exit the back of the van and run into a couple buildings only a few hundred yards away. John's squad was ordered to clear out the buildings as Second Squad was directed to secure the van. John informed his men, and they began to patrol up to the buildings.

Gunfire erupted from the building, and Lance Corporal Vasquez was shot in the throat as he stood next to John. The men hit the deck and began returning suppressive fire as the Navy doc and John tried to save the young Marine's life. Vasquez had been shot in the jugular and died within seconds. His hands covered in blood, John ordered Private First Class Jimento to take his AT-4—an 84 mm unguided, portable, single-shot recoilless rifle—and hit the building as John shot several of his 30 mm high explosive / dual purpose grenades (HEDP) at the building.

As the gunfire ceased from the building, John and his Marines began to advance to the nearly destroyed structure. Since it was mostly made of dirt, the explosive rounds had done a lot of damage. Just outside the building, John took a grenade and yelled "Grenade!" as he threw it into the building to kill any possible survivors before they entered. The men got down before the explosion and entered the building following the explosion.

Several gunshots were heard as they cleared the small building, and then there was silence. Five enemy fighters not dressed in Iraqi uniforms lay dead within the building—some of them in pieces, others with their bodies bullet ridden. The blood covered the floor and what was left of some of the walls. There wasn't much left, and yet John had zero fucks to give because he had lost one of his men.

Once the buildings were declared secure, First Squad arrived and relieved John's squad to recover Vasquez's body. Once they had recovered the body, John and his squad returned to their positions to conduct battle damage assessment (BDA) of his men. With the exception of the death of Vasquez, the men in John's squad were accounted for with none wounded. At least the war for Vasquez was over, and he was going to go home. Some Marines that get killed never have a chance to go back home, in a box or otherwise.

John cleaned the blood off his hands with his canteen of water, ordering his men to top off on ammo and get ready for taking the city tomorrow. For the remainder of the night, the desert once again turned quiet and peaceful. Still running high off adrenaline, he could not sleep, although his body needed to. To ensure that his men got as much sleep as they could, he and his team leaders took the last watch. Alone with his thoughts, John began to think about his family, Amber, and Susan. He was sure they all missed him and wondered where he was and whether he was safe.

The sun began to rise, and John could hear Arabic singing calling for morning prayer over a loudspeaker emanating from the city. As his men began to wake up, the doc came over to John.

"You've been hit, John," he said as he began inspecting John's right arm. Due to the high adrenaline John had experienced and the darkness of night, John hadn't realized he was bleeding.

After taking his gear and jacket off, he saw that it was only a graze on his arm. Not wanting to be evacuated to the rear, John told the doc to just patch it up since it was only a flesh wound and that he would be OK.

"After we take the city, I'll make sure to have it taken care of," John reasoned.

"OK, make sure you do," the doc responded.

Artillery fire directed toward the city reminded everyone what they were about to face. Their faces, worn and tired, still held the same resolve to do their best as Marines; none of them showed fear. Whatever fate had in store for them was going to happen regardless. They were going to meet it head on and face it like men. Aircraft overhead launched missiles at selective targets within the city. They were "softening" it up before the infantry went in and cleared each building—block by block, room by room.

Loading into their trucks, John and his men proceeded to the outskirts of the city. As they arrived, in another part of the city, heavy small-arms gunfire and explosions were heard. Word on the radio was another battalion, 1st Battalion, 2nd Marines (1/2), within John's Marine Task Force, had come under heavy attack. The battalion had tried to take two bridges spanning the Euphrates River defended by Fedayeen and Ba'ath Party guerrilla soldiers. John's unit off-loaded from its trucks and began its assault on the city. Meeting no resistance, the Marines still maintained an alert state of awareness as they began to clear the outskirts of the city. The battle to take the city had begun.

Clearing house after house, John and his men only encountered civilians and families. Every Marine was disciplined with their weapons, and no civilian casualties were yet inflicted. In war, however, civilian casualties are inevitable. That is one of the many terrible outcomes of war. Percussion waves could be felt and heard as AH-1

Cobras fired hellfire missiles on enemy strongpoints and resistance increased.

As John and his men continued to clear buildings, they began to receive sniper fire and resistance from buildings across the street. As they returned fire, RPGs began exploding near them. Taking cover before they exploded, the men quickly returned fire and called for additional close air support (CAS). The world seemed to be on fire as bullets and RPGs impacted the building, pinning John and his men down.

With the Marines unable to launch their AT-4s at the other building and with CAS unavailable at the time, John grabbed his squad and decided to clear the three-story building from which they were receiving the most gunfire. As the squad made their way across the street, First and Second Squad laid heavy suppressive fire to cover John and his squad's movements. Upon their entry, the first floor was cleared. Just as they had trained to do, the Marines made their way up the stairs, where they began receiving gunfire.

Grenades were tossed into the room directly in front of the stairwell. Once the explosions were heard, the Marines cleared the other three rooms on the second floor. John and a couple of his Marines made a button-hook right into the second room as the second fireteam made entry into the room and the grenade went off. The third fireteam breached the third room on the left, while two Marines maintained security on the stairwells to the first and third floors.

Gunfire erupted from both sides. John shot one fighter in the left cheek, and the bullet exited the back potion of his head, leaving a spray pattern of blood on the wall. Another fighter came after him and began fighting John hand to hand. John was pinned to the ground fighting for his life. A couple of the Marines were able to pull the fighter up after beating him with their rifle butts; John took out his bayonet and stabbed him through the throat and into his skull.

Covered in blood, John pushed the dead fighter off him and retrieved his weapon. There were only two fighters in each room, all of whom were killed. Ensuring there was a full magazine loaded, he regrouped with his squad to take the third floor. As they made their way up to the third floor, more shots impacted above their heads in the stairwell. A couple more grenades were tossed, and as soon as the explosion was heard, they assaulted the third floor.

The third floor was one large, wide room. In the center of the room, a dead fighter's body riddled with shrapnel lay lifeless in a puddle of blood next to his sniper rifle. The room was cleared, and the building was secured. Before leaving the building, John recovered a medal and a wooden folded knife inside the pocket of one of the fighters he had killed. He grabbed a second medal from the other fighter, the one he had stabbed in the throat. These were his war trophies. John didn't know how many people he had killed so far, but he had at least two confirmed kills.

John and his unit continued clearing the city, building by building, room by room, until the sun began to set. They had cleared an area large enough to provide security. Here they could sleep in a building for the first time in what seemed like months before resuming operations the next day. Surprisingly, as the men began to settle into their positions for the night, a welcomed sight was seen. Two large, orange mail bags were delivered. They were about to receive mail for the first time since they had left Kuwait.

The letters and packages for Vasquez were taken out and left to the side to be returned to his family in the States. John received one package from Amber, one letter from Susan, and several letters from his mother, sister, and grandparents. John immediately opened the package from Amber and found several packs of cigarettes, candy, and snacks. It had been a while since he had had a cigarette. He had run out of the bloody cigarettes a couple days ago. He was surprised to receive only one letter from Susan and decided to open that one last.

The letters from his family told him that they were proud of him and supported him while he was over here. Everyone was praying and wondering where he was and whether he was OK. His mother tried to insert humor into her letters with jokes and told him what they had been up to. He could tell she was worried because she hadn't received any letters from him. She asked him to please write, just so she would know that he was all right. He was sure that they had already received his letters well before he received theirs, that at least they knew he was alive when he sent them.

Tears began to fill his eyes as he thought about how devastated his mother would be if he were killed. *This is not the time to think about all that right now*, he reasoned with himself. He'd save that for another day, when he had time to think about all of it. Should the worst happen, and he did die, then there would be nothing he could really do about that. He had accepted his fate, and if that meant death, then so be it. John considered himself already a dead man walking, so if he lived through all of this, he would be one of the lucky ones.

He held the last letter in his hand. The posting address read "Susan McIntyre" and indicated a new home address in Alabama. John got a sick feeling in his stomach as he held and examined the letter, not sure whether to open it.

I might as well just get this over with, he thought to himself.

He knew exactly what this letter was, and it was not a letter anyone would want to receive in the middle of a war. He opened the letter and read "Dear John." He burst out laughing at the hilarity of reading a Dear John letter addressed to a guy named John. A couple Marines in his unit had already received their Dear John letters; *it's my turn to receive one*, he thought.

Dear John,

I have been watching the news, and it's so terrible what's going on. How have you been? I hope you're OK and doing well, all things considered. I've thought a lot about our time together—the fun times we shared—and I hope when this is all over you make it back home safe and in one piece. I know it has to be rough on you as it has been rough on me as well. I've felt so lonely these past couple months since I haven't seen you since the beginning of October, just before you shipped out. Why wouldn't you see me before you left?

You don't have to answer, as that doesn't matter anymore. My feelings for you have changed. I know I messed up when we first met, and I broke up with you. You were never the same with me again, and I understand why. What I have to tell you is not easy for me, and this will be the last letter you will receive from me. I wasn't pregnant with your baby, John. I wanted so desperately to marry you that I would have done anything to make that happen.

I haven't seen you since October and wouldn't see you until you got back, if you get back. I knew you would figure out that I lied to you and would have ended things with me anyway. I have met a really great guy at my church, and we just got married two weeks ago (hence my new last name). I'm pregnant with our first child, for real this time;and we are very happy.

I hope that one day you meet a woman worthy of you because I want you to be happy, John. I know this is not something you wanted to receive in the mail over there, but it's better to find out now than find out when you get back home. I'm so sorry for everything, and I hope one day you can forgive me and we can still just be friends. Please be safe and take care. I wish you nothing but the best.

P.S. Please don't write me back.

Love,

Susan McIntyre

John held the letter for a few moments, reading and rereading it in disbelief. He wasn't overly hurt or surprised by the fact that Susan had found and was married to another man. John knew it had only been a matter of time before she would find someone new. Although she talked about being Christian and her love for God, she enjoyed dick way too much to be faithful to only one man.

Welp, he's going to need a lot of luck in that marriage. I wonder if he really is the father? He laughed to himself.

The one thing that did bother John was the fact that for months he had thought that he was going to be a father. He was planning to leave the Marines, get a normal job, raise a family. All of that had been shattered with this letter.

How could she lie to me like that, he thought. *Did she not think I was going to find out?*

Seeing John staring at the letter, Staff Sergeant Steele came over and said, "Everything OK, Sergeant Devereaux?"

"Yes, Staff Sergeant, I'll be fine. Just some bad news from home is all."

"Yeah, that happens sometimes in war. It even happened to me the first time I was here during the first Persian Gulf War."

Staff Sergeant Steele began to explain further without John having inquired about what had happened. "I was a young PFC in my first infantry unit. I had married my high school sweetheart, and I thought we were going to grow old together. Turns out the military and marriage do not mix. We get deployed for God knows how long, and they get bored and lonely back home, which is a recipe for disaster. A little while into my deployment, I got a letter in the mail like you. She said that she was leaving me, taking my kid, and that she never wanted to see me again because we were through." He paused to take a drag of his cigarette.

Then he continued. "I haven't seen my daughter in years. She doesn't even know me, because my ex-wife claims I was abusive to her and our daughter. So the courts gave her full custody. She of course married some other guy and then divorced him as well. I'm not about being in your business, Sergeant, just putting things into perspective. If the Corps wanted you to have a wife, they would have issued one.

"But seriously, one thing my old platoon sergeant told me that's helped me out a lot—and I hope it helps you out: she's never yours; it's just your turn."

"Or I was never hers, and it was just her turn," John quipped back. They both laughed, and John thanked him for the advice.

Both men finished their cigarettes and settled in for some much-needed sleep, even if it was for just a couple hours. The sun would be coming up soon. John was kind of surprised Staff Sergeant Steele would share something like that with him, because Staff Sergeant Steele was widely known for being a hard-ass. John thought about what he had said, and it made sense as he pondered their encounter. *I'll have time to think about that tomorrow,* he thought as he drifted off to sleep.

The Marines began waking up before the sun began to rise. That meant a short amount of time to make sure their weapons were clean, ensure their magazines were topped off, and eat some chow before they resumed clearing operations.

This is going to be a long day, John thought as he made sure he and his men were ready.

Staff Sergeant Steele and Lieutenant Smith briefed the squad leaders on which buildings needed to be secured that day. "Good job yesterday, BTW," Staff Sergeant Steele stated as he looked at John. "Ready for another round?"

"My Marines and I are always ready, Staff Sergeant," John responded.

Their mission began with a patrol in the streets. First Squad took the left side, Second Squad took the right side, and John's squad was halved between the left and right sides, providing rear security. The patrol stopped for a moment, and all of the Marines took a knee. John took this time to adjust his comms gear, so he took his helmet off. Nobody saw the RPG impact near him. The explosion took everyone by surprise as they sought cover. John was lying down in the street.

Several Marines came to John and dragged him to safety; his face was covered in blood. The doc came and asked John if he was OK. Due to the percussion, John couldn't hear anything. Shrapnel had pierced his left ear and cut open his left cheek, and there was another gash under his right eye.

"You're one lucky motherfucker," the doc exclaimed as he pulled out the shrapnel and bandaged the wounds on John's face.

First Squad went into the building, and within minutes gunfire erupted. John remained on the ground as his Marines provided security. Sporadic shots were fired at the Marines from the surrounding buildings.

John told the doc, "We're going to get these men off the street and patch me up, then." He then gave an order to Corporal Johnson. "See that building? Secure it. We're going to go in there!"

Doc and Private Lawson grabbed John, and as the Marines cleared the building, they entered.

The building appeared abandoned and empty, Corporal Johnson advised Staff Sergeant Steel and Lieutenant Smith, who were in the adjacent building. The doc poured a canteen of water over John's face and patched him up. John tried to get up, and the doc said, "Sit the fuck down till I'm done with you."

"Fuck you. I'm not out of this for some bullshit," John responded. He stood up, and after clearance from the doc, he joined the platoon in the adjacent building.

Having regrouped, the Marines exited the building on high alert, ready for further contact. As they patrolled down the streets, everyone's eyes were focused on the windows and rooftops, looking for more enemy fighters. The Marines could sense something was wrong since all of the civilians remained off the street. None of the shops were open, and no traffic was on the street. During their patrol, gunfire once again erupted from the rooftops.

As the Marines reengaged, John got a lucky shot at one of the rooftop fighters and killed him instantly. The firefight only lasted for a few moments. Several of the fighters were killed, and none of the Marines in John's unit received any casualties. The remainder of the patrol was uneventful, and the Marines set up defensive positions, settling in for the evening. Since most of the Iraqi resistance in the city had been subdued, the focus of the battle shifted from full combat to cordon-and-search operations.

COMBAT OPERATIONS CONCLUDE

After a few days of patrolling without further enemy contact, John and his unit received orders to continue north toward An Numaniya. Their mission was to conduct security checkpoints along the highway, since Nasiriyah had been declared secure, although random uncoordinated attacks by Iraqi Fedayeen continued. As they continued north, John and his men wondered what was in store for them next.

Shockingly, along the road stood dozens of civilians waving and smiling at the Marines as they pressed forward. Some Marines threw candy to the children but were ever so aware that they were not completely out of danger.

"Make sure you keep an eye on their hands and on the horizon," John told his men. He did not want them to be complacent, especially now that they were seeing cheering, happy faces. They still had a job to do, and they were not finished with it just yet.

Arriving in Numaniya, John and his men set up in an old, abandoned school. Between the three companies of Marines, they established a security checkpoint on the highway. Their mission was to inspect all vehicles and people traveling on the road. John had seen whole trunks full of cigarettes, camels on the beds of trucks, coffins on top of car roofs, and severely wounded civilians either burned or missing limbs trying to get away from the fighting.

One such scene that John would never forget involved a young girl no older than six riding on a bus from Baghdad, the majority of her body severely burned and peeling away. John knew she wasn't going to make it much longer and asked doc to check her out. With only so many supplies, there was only so much that doc could do. To this day John doesn't know if she survived, but inside his heart he certainly hopes she did.

John and his unit remained in Numaniya until the middle of May, the same month in which President Bush declared the end of "major combat operations." Aside from manning the security checkpoint, there wasn't any further contact with the enemy. Their mission had become routine, and they wanted to go home. Soon enough another unit arrived and assumed responsibility of the security checkpoint. John was about to start his journey back.

Although he was happy that he was about to head back to the States, inside he remembered how he had wanted to die a hero in combat, which hadn't happened. There was a piece of him that would always remain in Iraq. He had killed. Taken human lives, even if it was in self-defense and part of his job as a Marine. Every time John closed his eyes, he remembered his dead friends and the people he had killed—the bodies of civilians strewn about, the destruction he was a part of. In the moment of battle, he didn't have to think, just react. Now that he was heading back home, he had all the time in the world to think. For the rest of his life, he would have time to think back at what he had done, what he had experienced. This is why many men never truly come home.

Having returned to Kuwait, John's unit was going to reboard the USS *Kearsarge*, the ship that had brought John over here; it was also the ship Amber was on. He was excited to see Amber once again. He hadn't seen her since the middle of February, and he knew that so much of him had changed in the three months since.

After all their ammunition was turned in, John held an empty rifle for the first time in months. They had to wait a couple days in Kuwait before boarding the *Kearsarge*. John and his men took advantage of this downtime to get some much-needed sleep. The men were still filthy, having not showered or changed their clothes in months; they didn't care. They would get a change of clothes and hot showers when they got back on the ship.

After a couple days, John and his unit were transported back to the *Kearsarge* via CH-46 helicopters. When they arrived, the sailors gagged and held their breath as the Marines walked through the passageways to their sleeping areas. John laughed at the sailors' reactions, as the sailors had no clue what the Marines had been through while in Kuwait and Iraq. Although he did not see Amber on his way, he wanted to see her when he was showered and in a clean uniform.

After a long-needed shower and now in a new uniform, John went to the smoke deck and lit his first cigarette on-ship. Just as he was about to take another puff, Amber asked, "Mind if I join you, Marine?"

John turned and looked at her with a smile. "Sure. Is there enough room for the both of us?" They laughed and began talking about their respective experiences while apart. John didn't mention anything that he had done or that he had killed people—just light conversation.

"Thank you for the care packages and letters, by the way; they meant a lot to me," John stated.

"You're welcome. I wish I could have sent you more, but there was only so much we could send at one time. I'm not going to lie, John, I was incredibly scared that something might have happened to you over there. I spent so many nights awake thinking about you and what you were going through," she responded. John smiled but remained silent, slightly touching her hand, comforting her.

As the voyage made its way back to the States, John and Amber resumed having sex aboard the ship and anytime they were both free (to make up for lost time, of course). They made promises to see each other when they got back, to keep in touch, just before John debarked from the ship and returned to Camp Lejeune.

The welcome back was like that of all other deployments John had experienced. Marines and families hugged and cried, happy the Marines were home safe. Like after his other two deployments, John had returned home a combat veteran, more medals and ribbons on his chest—with no welcome home.

He didn't really care about all of that. In a few days, he was going to go on leave for a couple weeks and visit his family.

John was excited to see them and thanked them for the letters and packages. His mother cried when she saw John, inspecting his face, scared of the shrapnel he had received in Nasiriyah. He was welcomed home as a hero, but John felt like anything but. He knew he had two months left on his contract before he could take terminal leave or reenlist in the Marines. The choice was his to make. He just didn't know which direction to take.

CHAPTER 6

S itting in his barracks room, John was contemplating getting out of the Marines. He loved the Marine Corps, even though sometimes the bullshit could drive him insane. His relationship with Amber was becoming more serious as they maintained long-distance communication. Amber was stationed at Naval Station Norfolk in Virginia, and he remained at Camp Lejeune. As their relationship progressed, John began to think about a life outside the Marines, pursuing a civilian career. He knew marriage and the military did not mix. In order to pursue the relationship, John chose to end his career in the Marines.

Because John only possessed infantry and special operations skills, the only real job he could transfer those skills to was that of police officer. The application process would take months, yet John was convinced that he should pursue a career as a police officer.

John's chain of command was not happy when he told them he was going to pursue this career. Although a short-timer, John applied to the Newport News Police

Department to get the process started before he got out. His plan was to move to Newport News, Virginia, become a police officer, and move in with Amber. He wanted to start a life and have a family. The morning John was due to get out of the Marines, his command decided to conduct a surprise urinalysis. He was only a couple hours from going to the admin office to pick up his DD-214 (separation paperwork) and head to Virginia.

"But I'm getting out this morning; why do I need to piss in a cup?" John asked Staff Sergeant Steele.

"Because you're still a Marine in this command, and you will piss in a cup before you get out," Steele barked.

After pissing in the cup, John walked over to the admin building and received his DD-214. Having out-processed earlier, John got into his prepacked car and left the front gate of Camp Lejeune with a huge smile on his face as he made his way up to Virginia.

Arriving in Virginia, John met up with Amber. They had already reserved an apartment for when he arrived. The only thing she had to do was go to her old apartment to retrieve a couple items. When they arrived at her old apartment, she opened the door, and her face turned pale white. John looked at her and asked her what was wrong. She was silent as another man appeared in the doorway.

"So, this is who you are leaving me for, huh?" the guy asked.

John looked at him and said, "What are you talking about? What do you mean 'who she is leaving you for'? We've been together for several months."

"Oh, wow, she didn't tell you that we were together?"

"No, I had no idea she was seeing you, bro. This is all news to me."

John was pissed he had left the Marines for this woman who apparently was seeing another man. Initially there was silence; she collected her things as John and her ex stood silently in the doorway.

"Take your shit and leave, bitch; get the fuck out of my house," he yelled at Amber. With her things gathered, Amber and John began walking to his car.

"Fucking bitch," the guy repeated as he followed John and Amber to his car. "You better watch out for her because she will do the same thing to you."

Trying to deescalate the situation, John remained quiet. The ex pushed Amber before they reached the car, and she tripped. John and her ex began to fight and roll on the ground, destroying a small bush in the process. John stood up as Amber's ex lay on the ground.

"Don't fucking touch her, or I will fuck you up more," John warned.

John and Amber returned to the car and put her things inside. As they drove off to their new apartment, her ex dusted himself off and walked back into the house. Internally John was pissed at Amber as they rode in silence to their apartment. John needed time to think about what he was going to say. He hoped she had a good reason for what he had just witnessed.

I just got out of the military, and I'm in the hiring process to become a police officer, John reasoned with himself.

When they arrived at the apartment and unloaded the car, John asked Amber, "So what the fuck was that all about? How long have you been seeing him? Did you have sex with him while you were with me? Why didn't you tell me about this before I got out of the military and moved up here?"

"I broke up with him back in January, before I met you on deployment. He was just living there until he could get his own place."

"Did you have sex with him?"

"Yes, but only one time a couple months ago. We were drunk, and I made a big mistake. Please forgive me, John," Amber pleaded.

John needed time to process everything that had happened and decide what to do now—break up with her and continue to pursue his career as a police officer, reenlist in the Marines, or stay with her and work things out. In a decision John would ultimately regret, he made the decision to forgive Amber and give her the benefit of the doubt.

I love her, and I think we can make this work, he said to himself. So John and Amber stayed together and lived in the apartment. He worked as a loss prevention specialist at a retail store while Amber still had a couple years remaining on her enlistment contract with the Navy. During a car ride toward Norfolk, Amber proposed the idea of getting married so they could collect additional money through the military's basic allowance for housing (BAH) (many people in the military get married just for the BAH benefits).

Another mistake that would long haunt John—the biggest mistake of his life—was agreeing to marry Amber.

They certainly needed the money. In a small ceremony at a judge's house, John and Amber were married by the justice of the peace. John knew the moment he said "I do" that he had made the wrong decision.

LIFE IN THE POLICE DEPARTMENT

Everything remained pretty calm in the months following the wedding. John continued through the hiring process for the Newport News Police Department, taking a battery of written, psychological, and physical tests (and passing each one with flying colors). He also appeared before a board of police officers and faced questions about why he wanted to be a police officer. Having proven himself an outstanding candidate to be a police officer, John was hired by the department. Amber remained in the Navy, undergoing several small deployments, and was excited to learn that John was going to be a police officer.

Life seemed to be going as planned. He was set to become a police officer, he was married, and life seemed stable. Sure, John and Amber had their arguments, but they were not like the fights of his childhood.

John attended a one-week preacademy session to prepare police recruits for the four-month police academy. Because his department didn't have their own police academy, John attended the Hampton Roads Criminal Justice Training Academy, which happened to be in Newport News. The first day of training, recruits from multiple police departments in the region were formed up like in the military. Being a paramilitary organization, the police attract many veterans from the military branches. It's much like being in a military organization without being in the military.

Of course, the instructors from various police departments had to establish their authority over the recruits (another similarity with the military). After the recruits were introduced to the instructors, the hazing session began. It was laughable that all the instructors, despite their pretenses of authority, had a large gut, were clearly out of shape, and could obviously not do the exercises they were having the recruits do.

John was still very physically fit from being in the Marines, and so the exercises were almost ridiculous to him. After a couple hours of exercising, the recruits settled in for classes. They were going to study a variety of subjects, but they started with case law and the law more generally. Historically, the academic portion of the curriculum is the most challenging and compels a lot of students to drop out during the first week of academy. Students were required to pass the test with a score of 100 percent. If they took an exam and failed, they were tested once again on the questions that were missed. If those questions weren't answered correctly, they had one final exam. If they didn't pass that time, they were dropped from the academy.

John was taught a variety of subjects once he completed the academics portion of the academy. During his four months of training at the academy, he learned how to conduct criminal investigations via mock crime scenes, patrol procedures, firearms training, traffic control, defensive driving, self-defense tactics, emergency vehicle operations, basic first aid, and interrogation methods, all the while conducting physical training every day. Although this process was longer than Marine basic training, John was able to go home at the end of the day, and the four-month academy went by quickly.

Once John completed the police academy, he accomplished his goal of becoming a police officer. Although still a rookie, he had to attend additional training at a five-week, in-house postacademy. His new instructors were experienced officers who had become trainers in the department. The postacademy taught the newly graduated recruits about Newport News Police standard operating procedures (SOP), while honing and reinforcing the training they had received at the academy.

The five-week course was not very difficult, although it was more physically challenging than the academy. Upon completion of the postacademy, John was sent to the South Precinct (the department is divided into three precincts—South, Central, and North) to complete his three-month field training period. During field training, John would take everything he learned in his previous training and apply it to real-world situations, all under the supervision of his field training Officer (FTO).

The South Precinct had a reputation for being in the roughest part of the city. The officers often joked that three months of FTO training in the South Precinct would expose a new rookie to more situations than an officer working a year in the other precincts. Much like in the military, here each precinct thought its precinct was the best. Arguably both the North and South Precincts were considered high-crime and high-drug areas.

Being in field training exposed John to a lot of experiences he had never had before. It was very different from his experience in the military. He was working in a very low-income area where the police were hated and despised. This exposure to inner-city life showed John how important his months of training would be. Preparedness was a matter of life or death. He realized how quickly everything could go south if he was not cautious and alert.

As a police officer, you never know when a traffic stop will turn deadly or when a call for service might injure you or end your life. The potential for danger lurks every time officers report for duty. It's well known among officers that the most dangerous incidents for them are traffic stops and domestic disturbance calls.

When a police officer initiates a traffic stop, he has no idea whom he is encountering. Therefore officers are very cautious when approaching a vehicle. They place their fingerprints on the back of the vehicle, just in case something happens to them. In domestic disturbance calls, emotions run high between the parties, and as a result, sometimes irrational thoughts cross their minds. Officers can take every precaution available to them, but in the end they're not in control of someone else's actions.

During John's field training period, he became more proficient at traffic stops, applying criminal and traffic law without having to refer to his cheat sheet. He refined his report writing and his ability to conduct criminal investigations and overall increased his knowledge in applying the law to certain situations. He learned how to properly collect and catalogue evidence while simultaneously learning everything about the area he was assigned to work in, gaining invaluable experience in preparation for riding alone in his own patrol vehicle.

As John was a rookie in training, his FTO would ensure he received the maximum amount of exposure to various situations. He had to complete a checklist of training and law enforcement activities before he would be given approval by the department to ride solo. One of John's first calls for service as a trainee on FTO was his also his first dead body call.

Upon arrival to the scene in mid-November, John and his FTO walked into an apartment where an elderly man had died of natural causes on the carpet, in the center of his living room. Because there was no ventilation and the man had been dead for several days, there was an incredibly putrid smell of death in the air. John's FTO advised him that he would get used to the smell and to avoid leaving the apartment. He advised John would more than likely throw up upon reentering the apartment if he did leave.

John was told to inspect the body to make sure that there were no signs of injury before the funeral home came to retrieve it. John was accustomed to death and the morbid. Seeing a dead body didn't faze him in the least, especially after he had personally taken human lives. To him this was just part of the job. Rolling the body over, he noticed a lot of bruising on the back. His FTO told him that's what "pooling" looks like.

He explained, "When a person dies in a certain position, there is no blood circulating in the body. Gravity takes over and presses downward, so the blood concentrates in one area. That's why they call it *pooling*. So, for example, he died on his back. That's why the blood is collected in the back. If he had died lying facedown, the blood would have pooled to his chest and face."

After John completed his field training period, he was released to ride solo, although even then the dispatchers made sure to send John veteran officers to back him up on calls. He may have been done with training, but he had much to still learn. At least by now he was a semi-effective police officer; time and experiences were his teachers now. The amount of authority and responsibility is immense for a law enforcement officer. Split-second decisions can become matters of life and death. That is why it's vital for law enforcement officers to receive such extensive training.

Law enforcement officers have to dissociate themselves from any situation and not think of victims or the dead as people. Although there are plenty of videos showing cops with overinflated egos, the humanism aspect is detrimental to being an effective police officer. It's nothing personal but a coping mechanism since law enforcement officers are subjected to the worst society has to offer day in, day out. It is very easy to become jaded, and that's why gallows humor is used to add levity to hard situations.

If a law enforcement officer took things personally or thought too much about what he witnessed on any given shift, he would go crazy. Because of John's upbringing and his experiences in the Marines, he was never very close to people and considered himself a social outcast at the expense of his humanity. This disassociation with reality and his ability to keep these experiences contained to work gave John an objective outlook and an unbiased opinion of any situation he was presented with.

And John was presented with many crazy and intense situations. He was a rookie who had grown up in the country and was now working in an inner-city neighborhood. It was a stark contrast to the life he had lived up to that point, and he certainly had a learning curve to overcome. It would just take more time and experience for him to develop himself into the best police officer he could be. Luckily, he had the strong mentorship of veteran officers on his shift.

Working the evening shift from 3:00 p.m. to 1:00 a.m., John experienced policing at its busiest time. Day shift officers had to handle break-ins or the occasional drug dealer. Since most people go to work, there is not a lot that really happens during this period. The calls for service increase substantially during the evening shift, especially since this shift is more often than not undermanned. There was one evening during which only four officers, including John, were on patrol in one of the roughest parts of the city.

Calls for service including domestic assaults, gun and drug activity, suspicious persons, assaults, juvenile delinquents, runaways, and the like were all too common. It was usually near the end of shift that calls for service would include shootings, stabbings, maiming, trespassing, and DUIs. Those calls alone would occupy their time and divert their attention from patrolling the neighborhoods. Incidents like these would also ensure an end time past 1:00 a.m.

In early May 2005, John was approaching the one-year mark of his time with the police department. Although still considered new to the department, he had gained enough valuable experience to be an effective police officer in his area. Around 9:00 p.m. he was dispatched to the Speedy Mart convenience store in his area to investigate a person selling stolen items on the property.

Upon arrival John observed two men carrying black duffle bags in their right hands walking away from the store. In order to prevent the men from leaving the area—they matched the description on the call—he parked his vehicle near the intersection, and then he initiated contact with them.

As he exited his vehicle, he instructed both men to stop and asked to see their identification. John was on his own, his backup minutes away; one of the men left the area, having disregarded John's instructions. John maintained contact with the male that remained and advised dispatch of the clothing description of the male departing the area so that other police units would be on the lookout. As John was on the radio, the male began pacing, attempting to leave the area. As he walked away, John advised his backup that the suspect was not following his commands and he needed assistance.

The suspect continued to disregard John's instructions, and John advised him that he was under arrest for obstruction of justice, refusing to provide identification, and preventing John from conducting a thorough criminal investigation. As John attempted to arrest the suspect, the suspect became combative, pushing John away, attempting to prevent his arrest. Because the soft empty hand control techniques had not worked, John elevated his use of force and deployed his department-issued oleoresin capsicum (OC) spray, spraying the suspect in his eyes at a distance of about three feet.

The OC spray had no effect on the suspect as he charged and pushed John, knocking the can out of his hands; the can landed in the road as John fell to the ground. The suspect ran into the middle of the road and stopped. John advised dispatch that he was in a foot pursuit and the suspect was becoming combative.

John instructed the suspect to get out of the road for his safety. He attempted to physically subdue the suspect once again, and they got into another physical altercation. The altercation continued across the street from the store parking lot. This is when the suspect grabbed John by his uniform shirt, lifted him up, and threw him to the ground.

John's head bounced off the pavement; the back of his head split open on the sidewalk, causing him to black out for a second or two. Regaining his bearing, John attempted to deploy his collapsible baton as the suspect attempted to gain control over John's holstered pistol. John struck the suspect several times; he let go of John's pistol and began running away. John continued to chase the suspect, the back of his head open and bleeding, a garbage can having been thrown at him. An officer-in-distress call was initiated citywide. All available units in the whole city were heading as fast as they could to John's location.

John continued to chase the suspect, who had broken into an occupied apartment building and thrown an unoccupied baby playpen at John. After they exited the residence, another physical encounter ensued. John had to once again use his baton on the suspect. As officers began to arrive on scene, the suspect surrendered and was arrested. One of the officers noticed the back of John's head bleeding and called for a medic at his location.

As the suspect was being transported to jail, John was transported to the hospital, where he received several staples to the back of his head. It was later determined the suspect had been high on heroin during the encounter. This must have been why the suspect didn't feel pain when John used his OC spray and baton on him.

This was a very interesting time in John's life. John experienced regular traffic stops and learned a valuable lesson from another officer about such procedures. This officer had initiated a traffic stop on a vehicle. Because the female driver had not gotten a ticket, a formal complaint had been sent to the police department for sexual harassment. To avoid a situation like this, if John initiated a traffic stop, the driver more than likely got a ticket, regardless of gender.

Other extraordinary traffic stops involved high-speed pursuits of drivers dangerously speeding in school zones or transporting guns and drugs in their vehicles. John was more concerned about getting guns and drugs off the street, especially because of the earlier incident. During that incident, a concerned citizen eventually became a certified reliable informant for John. If this informant advised John or other officers about drug activity, the police had the authority to detain anyone matching the description given. Every case in which the informant was correct added to their reliability, which had to be continuously evaluated.

In addition to the traffic stops, there was a period of time during which John was known as "Doctor Death." It seemed like every call John went on was for someone who had either committed suicide, died of natural causes, or been murdered. John forgot about some of these incidents, but the ones he remembered certainly left an imprint. There was one man who had hanged himself with a belt in the closet. With the man still dangling in his trailer closet with his black tongue sticking out, John used his Leatherman tool to cut the wooden rod. As they lowered his body to the ground, gas from his body let out, releasing a God-awful stench that filled the trailer.

One call for service involved a six-month-old baby boy being smothered by his father. Another included a man who had died in bed of AIDS. One call involved a double murder, while another call involved a worried family that had not spoken to a relative in a few days. With an apartment key in hand to conduct a welfare check, John and his sergeant attempted to contact the resident. After repeated phone calls and knocks at the person's door, John and his sergeant made entry into the apartment, at which time they observed bloodstains on an interior wall. Both unholstered their pistols and began to room clear the apartment.

As they made their way through the kitchen, more bloodstains became evident on the kitchen floor. Blood had apparently been smeared by a hand along the hallway leading to the back bedroom. As John entered the master bedroom, he observed an unkempt bed with blood soaking the sheets and a two-liter 7UP bottle half full of clotted blood on the nightstand. Wondering what the hell was going on, the sergeant opened the bathroom door and found the tenant lying naked on the floor, his hand in the blood-covered toilet.

It was later determined through talking with relatives and confirmation with the medical examiner that the tenant had terminal lung cancer and had died of natural causes. Aside from all the blood throughout the house, nothing indicated there was any foul play involved. The family was heartbroken, something John had seen many times.

The amount of death and violence John had been subjected to through the Marines and within the police department effectively severed any emotional response. He was emotionally detached from society, and nothing he saw or observed could faze him—not even an incident in which a teen had been shot over a gang dispute, with John providing medical attention to him, watching him take his last breath. A mother taking her two-year-old daughter and placing her butt on a hot stove, the outlines of the burner rings permanently burned into her skin. Or the six-month-old baby struck in the arm during a drive-by shooting.

All of this insanity seemed to be commonplace and further toughened John's skin. He had seen countless murder victims. Most murdered over drugs, money, or gang-related disrespect. He encountered countless drug overdoses and victims of violence. The going saying within the shift, "Today's victim is tomorrow's suspect," had never held truer.

Often incidents would come unexpectedly. For instance, Officer Shelton and John would pull their cars up alongside each other and talk when they were taking a break from patrolling or about ready to get off a shift. One time they heard several gunshots near them. Initiating a patrol of the area, John and Officer Shelton observed a young teen male lying in the center of an intersection. The victim was not more than fifteen years old but had what would later be determined to be three shotgun holes in his back. As John began CPR and attempted to stop the bleeding, Officer Shelton notified dispatch of the situation and requested an ambulance. Soon a crowd of over a hundred people began to circle the officers as they waited for the ambulance.

Officer Shelton calmed the crowd, telling them they were doing everything they could for the young boy and they needed space to work. After what seemed like an eternity, the ambulance and other officers responding arrived on-scene. Unfortunately, the victim died at that spot. There was nothing John could have done to save his life.

A couple months later, another shooting occurred at the end of another shift as John and Officer Shelton conversed. Earlier in the day, John had received information from his informant about a man selling drugs in the area of the Speedy Mart. Having been given a full description, John observed the individual at the spot where the informant told him he would be standing. John stopped his vehicle and attempted to contact the suspect before the suspect took off; another foot pursuit initiated.

After only making it a block, the suspect was tackled in an empty parking lot covered in pea gravel. John had scraped the skin along his forearm. Bleeding, John still handcuffed the suspect and retrieved the heroin he was selling from his pockets. After he was bandaged up and the suspect transported to jail, John resumed his shift. He had taken a domestic assault call where a drunken man had opened his wife's right cheek with a broken beer bottle. Whenever she tried to talk, John could see the inside of her mouth.

After a long day of arrests, going back and forth from jail, securing evidence, and report writing, John was tired as he and Officer Shelton sat and talked about their crazy day. Gunshots rang out close by once again, and John and Officer Shelton laughed, telling each other they were bad luck together. When they arrived on-scene, yet another young teen male lay motionless on the ground surrounded by hundreds of people. The young man had been shot in the right ear, and the bullet had exited his right eye. Every time John did a CPR compression, blood squirted onto his arms, including the arm with the bandaged wound acquired earlier in the shift.

The ambulance and other police units arrived on-scene; John escorted the ambulance to the hospital. The young man was stable upon arriving at the hospital. During the investigation, it was learned he was an innocent bystander attending a high school graduation party. Apparently, he was going to be graduating high school the next day. He was a good student and had no known gang affiliations. He was just in the wrong place at the wrong time.

At the hospital the doctors informed his parents that the boy was in a coma and although they suspected he would never wake up, in any case he would be permanently brain damaged and deaf. He would never be the same young man his parents knew him to be. His family gave him peace as he was taken off life support. Although emotionally broken, the young man's parents thanked John at the hospital for doing everything he could to save their boy's life. It may have been a rough shift for John that night, but it was an even harder night for that young man and his parents, family, and friends.

John never had much luck with CPR, though at least amid the unpleasant opportunities he was faced with, he did the best he could. A third and final time John gave real-world CPR happened when a man had had a heart attack while driving. He had driven his truck into a utility pole. Upon John's arrival, the elderly driver lay hunched over his steering wheel, his body lifeless. John did not feel a pulse and began initiating CPR, but it was too late. The man was gone, but John did everything he could. What many people don't realize—when seconds count, the police are minutes away.

John continued to serve on the police department, although his reputation for being a "shit magnet" was quickly spreading throughout the department. It seemed like no matter what was happening, some officers got into a lot of crazy situations, while others couldn't find any if they tried. Having already had his head stapled back together, John experienced another physical injury while on the job.

A call for service indicated a large group of teens fighting—typical during the summer months. When John and the other units arrived, the teens began to scatter and run. All the officers began chasing the suspects, capturing some of them. When John tackled the suspect he was chasing, they fell to the ground. The suspect's body weight and John's body weight landed as John's thumb was extended. There was a snap, and the ligaments in John's thumb were severed.

It took a couple months for John to recover from his thumb surgery. He had to have two metal pins and two metal wires placed in order to reattach his thumb. His career in law enforcement was in danger because he was not sure if he would ever be able to hold a firearm again. After surgery and physical therapy, John was able to resume active status and returned to his shift in the South Precinct.

John tried to take it easier and stay out of the spotlight. He was already leading the department in use-of-force reports and citizen complaints, all of which had been investigated by his command and internal affairs, who had determined them to be unsubstantiated and his use of force justified.

Amid trying to stay low, John was patrolling his area before the end of shift when he came across a man riding a bike without lights (a violation of city code ordinance). All John was going to do was give him a warning and tell him to have lights put on his bike. As John attempted to make contact, the man on the bike began to flee, and yet again John was in a foot pursuit.

The chain on the suspect's bicycle came off as he fell in the middle of an intersection before fleeing on foot. As John chased him, the suspect threw a small handgun into the brushes, and John tackled him to the ground. After he was in handcuffs, it was later learned the suspect had outstanding warrants for his arrest—for robbery, abduction, carjacking, and using a firearm in the commission of a felony. John reasoned that's why he had run. This arrest was so big it even made the local newspaper.

With the amount of hours John was putting into the police department, his homelife suffered. When he wasn't at work, John was in court testifying as part of all his pending criminal, traffic, and juvenile and domestic relations (JDR) cases. It was not uncommon for John to be in court from 8:30 a.m. until noon, only to work his shift from 3:00 p.m. to 1:00 a.m. thereafter (though the shift often ran to 2:00 a.m., and as late as 5:00 a.m.).

Doing the math, there was not a whole lot of time for sleep in that schedule. And he had to go to court on his days off. When John went to court, charges would be dropped, dismissed, or plea-bargained away, so he had usually waited there for nothing. As explained earlier, when split-second decisions count, many law enforcement officers are sleep deprived.

No matter what John had done on his shift, he would come home to a nagging, unappreciative wife who regularly withheld sex from him because he was never around. So, John explained to Amber, "If you want to withhold sex from me, that's fine; I will get it from somewhere else."

There was no shortage of "badge bunnies" waiting to fuck a cop, mostly because it served their own interests; when they got pulled over, they could reference a cop's name and department, more times than not thus getting off without a citation. In any case, there were a number of dispatchers, female police officers, and civilians to choose from. John knew this and would not accept a sexless marriage. So he found sex elsewhere, with Amber's full knowledge. She had no problem with him getting what he needed from multiple other women.

John's sexless life began shortly after his first son was born (although John secretly questioned the validity of his son). During a shift John was working, he called Amber, who was visiting her family down in Florida. She answered the phone and told him she was visiting her family. Suspicious, John called her mother.

"Amber is out with friends right now; didn't she tell you?" her mother explained.

"No, she said she was with you guys, and I was making sure she was OK," John responded.

There was something wrong, and when he called her back, he confronted her about the situation. He told her he had already spoken with her family and had asked what she was doing.

"I'm out with friends," she responded.

"What friends? Why didn't you tell me the truth?" John questioned her.

He had seen a lot of this not only in the department but within the community in which he worked. This reminded him of a case he worked where he had been dispatched to a domestic violence call. The "victim" advised John and his partner that her husband had hurt her, showing a bruise on her arm. After getting the husband's information and obtaining a warrant for his arrest, John returned to her residence to provide an Emergency Protective Order (EPO), as is standard for all domestic violence cases.

When John arrived, a man who was not her husband answered and asked how he could help the officers. After determining he was not the suspect, the man advised John that he was the victim's boyfriend and was wondering what was going on. John talked to him as the "victim" received copies of the EPO paperwork. Through the investigation John learned that the boyfriend came over regularly and that day the victim's husband had taken off work unexpectedly. The "victim" had told her boyfriend that she would make sure her husband was out of the house for the night.

The suspect turned himself in and talked with John. John understood the situation at hand and took his statement as an objective third party. "There is already a warrant for your arrest—that I can do nothing about—but what I will do is testify to everything that I heard and observed at your house. I'm not against you in this; this isn't personal, and you're going to have to trust me," John explained. John felt uneasy about the whole situation and thought that this was more than likely a false claim, but he still had a job to do. This was the first innocent man that John knew internally to be innocent.

John experienced domestic violence at home with Amber, who even kicked and hit him; being a police officer, he kept it quiet. He didn't want his personal problems to affect his career. John did testify on behalf of the husband he arrested, and the case was dismissed. Whether the husband heeded that red flag warning or not, John never found out. He had his own red flags to deal with at home.

The sexless marriage and the verbal and physical abuse continued to be a constant strain on John. He tried to be the best father he could to a son he wasn't sure was his. An existential fear among men is raising a child that is not theirs. And even police officers can be subjected to domestic violence in the home. In order to avoid ridicule, many men face this situation alone. This is why there are more undocumented reports of domestic violence against men than documented ones. Men simply don't report it.

CHAPTER 7

After serving on the department for about four years, John had had enough. He had enough of the bullshit politics, the long hours on patrol and in court, the reduced retirement benefits as the city began to reduce costs. John tried out for the department's SWAT team, and during selection, it came down to Officer Shelton and John. Although John beat Officer Shelton in every test of endurance, and despite the fact that both he and Shelton had violated the tobacco policy implemented by the department, John was not selected—even after having carried Officer Shelton through half the course.

It's sometimes not what you know or how well you do; your reputation will always precede you. *Whom* you know can take you further than what you know in some cases, especially if you have a wide-ranging social circle. Many men get disheartened when they put their all into something and see no results. You have to learn to play the social politics game and learn from your failures. Dust yourself off and continue, no matter how many times you get knocked down. Social politics will always play a part in your life and future career aspirations.

Even after having received many accolades in the department, including the Police Chief's Award for Outstanding Contribution to Law Enforcement, John decided he was no longer passionate about being a police officer. After giving it careful consideration, John decided to reenlist in the Marines, where he could finish the remaining sixteen years of service and receive a full retirement package.

Although he would more than likely deploy several times again, career prospect–wise this was the best decision for him and his family. In the military John would have more opportunities to increase his education and skills to further his career, while simultaneously preparing himself for when he retired from the military.

Although the police department was already short manned, John resigned promptly. Because he was still within his individual ready reserve (IRR) time frame in the Marines, he was able to keep his rank of sergeant (still, he had to start his time in grade over like a newly promoted sergeant).

John accepted this as part of starting over. He regretted having gotten out in the first place, so this was a basic starting point for him to continue his career. He had further aspirations in the Marines, since this was going to be his career until retirement. John began to develop a long-term strategy for how he was going to accomplish his mission. He was in it for the long haul.

John's new strategy was to reenlist in the Marines, complete his bachelor's degree, become a Marine officer (because an officer's retirement is much better than a senior enlisted man's retirement), retire from the Marines, and join the CIA. Joining the CIA was also something John had wanted to do since he was a child. With his plan firmly in place, as part of his reenlistment, John changed his military career from infantry to the intelligence field with a guaranteed seat at the Army's Airborne School also known as jump school.

REENLISTING IN THE MARINES

The transition from police officer back to Marine was not all that difficult. He was still as physically fit as he had been during his first enlistment. This time, however, he was more mature and experienced. John chose the counterintelligence / human intelligence (CI/HUMINT) field because it was within the intelligence community. CI/HUMINT Marines were attached to infantry units when deployed; he would receive a Top Secret/ SCI clearance, and this would give him more experience interrogating and developing sources (akin to his experience in the police department working with confidential informants). John reasoned that this career path, along with his previous experience and an education, would make him an attractive candidate for the CIA.

While waiting for orders to report to his permanent duty station, John began preparing himself and his family for his eventual move back to Camp Lejeune. He had to get his house ready to sell; the housing market was doing poorly. Amber would have to remain in the area with their son, Corey, until the house sold. John would live as a geo-bachelor at his next duty station, making sure he had a place to move into when the house sold.

A month after his reenlistment, John received orders to report to the 2nd Intelligence Battalion in Camp Lejeune. He wasn't surprised, because it was the largest Marine Corps base on the East Coast. When he arrived, he checked into his unit and lived in the barracks once again, now as a geo-bachelor until his wife and son moved down. Nothing on the base had changed in the four years he had been gone. The faces looked younger, and the uniforms were different camo patterns, but everything else remained the same.

John's new unit was unlike his previous units in the infantry. It was composed of NCOs and SNCOs, with the lowest rank being a corporal. As a new sergeant in the unit, not having gone through the CI/HUMINT school, John was once again a new guy who had to prove himself to his peers and leadership. First, he had to go through job training, followed by waiting for his seat in jump school, before he would be able to complete the CI/HUMINT course. Marines who had not gone through the course were treated like boots Marines, no matter their rank or experience.

Starting over as a new sergeant without any leadership responsibility was a big change for John. It was a humbling experience being the new guy once again after having been a combat veteran and a police officer. He was used to leading Marines in combat, not being considered a junior Marine to be led. He knew it was going to take time to prove himself and be accepted within the unit. Whatever it took, he was going to complete his career goals.

The house in Newport News sold within a couple months of John arriving at Camp Lejeune. Amber and Corey moved into an apartment with John outside of base. He no longer had to live in the barracks, and his career in the Marines seemed more like a typical nine-to-five job, just in a military uniform. Because he was awaiting training, he had nondeployable status. As soon as he did complete the training, he would be deploying a lot. While awaiting training, John enrolled in an online school to complete his associate and bachelor's degrees. Everything was going as planned.

One day John received a call from his mother, who was crying on the other end of the phone. "Robert's gone. He cheated on me and got the other woman pregnant, so he just left me for her."

John tried to comfort her on the phone, but there was only so much he could do. "How about you sell the house and move down here for a fresh start?"

"I agree. I have to move out of here; there are just too many memories, John."

With a plan in place, his mother listed her home for sale as John found a place in Jacksonville ready for her to move into. A couple weeks later, his mom, Julie, Savanah, and Savanah's daughters moved down to Jacksonville.

John was happy his whole family was moving to be near him. It was the start of a new life in a new career with his family close by. John was happy to be able to see his family again on a regular basis. When his mother moved down, she was still a nervous wreck and very upset about what Robert had done to her. John tried to console her and resented Robert. Although there was nothing he could do, he helped his mother through the grieving process as best he could.

While waiting for his Top Secret clearance, a requirement of being in the CI/HUMINT community, to be adjudicated, John received orders to attend the three-week Army jump school located in Fort Benning, Georgia. Although John was afraid of heights, he was excited to attend the training and have a pair of jump wings pinned on his chest, something not very common in the Marines. Having made sure his family was set before he departed, he left Camp Lejeune and drove to Fort Benning.

After completing his in-processing at Fort Benning, John faced three weeks of airborne training broken down into ground week, tower week, and jump week. Living in old Army barracks from what seemed to be the 1950s, he was reminded of his days in boot camp. Even the airborne instructors, known as "black hats," attempted to be quasi drill instructors (known as drill sergeants in the Army). Having already been through Marine boot camp, John swallowed his ego and followed along with the training.

On the first morning of ground week, John and his fellow classmates—who numbered Marines, soldiers, and members of the other armed services—awoke at 4:00 a.m. to take the Army Physical Fitness Test (APFT). Before going to Fort Benning, John had to pass several Marine versions of the airborne test. The Marines version was designed to be harder. This ensured Marines attending the school were ready and would pass. It would be embarrassing for the Marine and the Marine Corps if they were to send someone who could not pass the APFT.

Ground week consisted of long days, physical exercise, and developing airborne skills and techniques. One of the skills consisted of learning how to land using mock doors and landing safely on the ground, also known as a parachute landing fall (PLF). Repetition was stressed to build muscle memory for jump week, when the trainees would actually jump out of airplanes. An incorrect PLF could result in broken bones or serious bodily injuries.

Once the PLF was completed satisfactorily from the mock doors, they transitioned to what is known as the swing ladder trainer (SLT). In this training tool, the trainee was in a harness, and the harness was hooked onto cables. The trainee would then lean off the platform and swing before the cables were unexpectedly released. This training provided a controlled falling environment, reinforcing proper PLF techniques.

Upon successful completion of the SLT, the trainee would practice jumping out a thirty-four-foot tower, which simulated jumping out of an aircraft. The trainee would be in a harness, as in SLT. When the trainee jumped out of the tower, he would ride a long cable to a berm where he would be caught by other trainees. The foot tower might not have seemed very high if viewed from the ground, but John observed some trainees unable to overcome their fear of heights standing at the exit door.

He felt his own sense of nervousness as he approached the door.

After the first week was completed and he was able to enjoy the weekend off, John maintained his online college studies. Monday was the beginning of his second week of training—tower week. This week was very important because in order to move forward to jump week, trainees had to qualify on SLT, complete mass exit exercise on the thirty-four-foot tower, meet all physical requirements, and successfully deploy from a 250-foot tower, gain canopy control thereafter, and land on the ground. John was hooked up to an open parachute held by rings. He was raised to the top of the tower, dangling 250 feet in the air. The view of the base was beautiful, and surprisingly the height of 250 feet was not as intimidating as that of the thirty-four-foot tower.

With an upward motion, the parachute released from the rings, and John maintained canopy control as he drifted to the ground. It was an exhilarating experience, one that only lasted a couple seconds. Doing a proper PLF, John landed safely on the ground. The only injury he observed among his classmates during this week was in an Army second lieutenant who did not do a proper PLF when he landed and broke his ankle. Unfortunately that was the end of training for the lieutenant. Confident going into jump week, John once again enjoyed a weekend to himself, still busy with the weekly online college assignments that were piling up.

Those who successfully completed tower week moved on to the final phase of training. This time they were going to be jumping out of planes at a height of about 1,250 feet. As the trainees were wearing parachutes that must have been issued in the 1950, John was nervous but confident he would be OK when jumping out of the plane. To successfully complete jump week, trainees had to complete five jumps at 1,250 feet from a C-130 or C-17 aircraft in varying conditions.

John had to complete a daytime "Hollywood" jump (where he only wore his helmet, harness, and reserve parachute), a nighttime "Hollywood" jump, a day combat jump, and a night combat jump (where along with his other equipment he had a rifle strapped to him and a thirty-pound rucksack between his legs). His fifth and final jump would be another night combat jump.

The first four jumps went great, although John decided that he preferred to keep his legs on the ground. When he first boarded the C-17, John tried to remain focused as he felt the nerves in his stomach churn. Anticipation of the unexpected encountered the fact that jumping out of a plane was now a reality. The noise was deafening as the doors of the C-17 opened. The trainees stood up and hooked up to the cable. The moment of truth—the green light was on, and the trainees were filing out the door. Without a moment's hesitation, John was out the door.

The deafening noise went away as he made his count to four and looked up thinking, *Check canopy; gain canopy control*. It was incredible how peaceful it was twelve-hundred-plus feet above the ground. Looking around the area, with their open canopies in close enough proximity, the trainees were talking to each other. The huge buildup of jumping from a plane released as John's nerves calmed. Falling for only about thirty seconds or so, John ensured that he was ready for a proper PLF. He had come too far to get injured and not complete his training. When he landed on the ground and recovered his parachute, he was happy he had successfully completed his first jump.

John's other three jumps were pretty much the same, with nothing really interesting happening—a good thing when jumping from a plane and landing on the ground, especially at night. John was only one jump away from completing jump school, and soon he would have his jump wings pinned to his chest. His final jump was going to be a night combat jump. All he had to do was jump out of the plane. His static line hooked up, standing at the door, John was ready to complete his final jump.

The green light turned on, and once again he shuffled outside the door of the C-17. As John jumped out, something didn't feel right. He had made it out of the plane but realized his risers were wrapped around his leg. Before he could untangle them, his parachute opened, and his leg snapped at the knee. Falling headfirst to the ground, John was able to pull down his riser enough to release his leg. With the release of the riser around his leg, his body snapped into the correct position, and his leg dangled, almost lifeless. He was saying, "Fuck. Fuck. Motherfucking fuck," all the way down. John realized he only had a few more seconds to release his gear before he landed.

Shortly after releasing his pack and weapon, John landed on the ground in excruciating pain. He didn't know what was wrong, only that he could not move his left leg. He began to shout for help, saying he was injured. One of the black hat instructors heard John and loudly yelled, "Shut the fuck up; this is a tactical zone!"

"Fuck you. I'm hurt!" John responded in pain.

The instructor ran over to John's location and with his flashlight saw John's predicament. "Holy shit," the instructor muttered as he saw John on the ground, his cord-wrapped leg unnaturally twisted on the ground.

The instructor called for a vehicle to pick John up and transport him to the medics. While waiting for the transport, the instructor began taking the equipment off John. John was in pain, but he also felt numb; the adrenaline was kicking into high gear. All John knew was that he could not move his leg from the knee down and that he was hurt pretty badly. To what extent, he didn't know.

The transport truck arrived, and several soldiers placed John in the bed along with his gear. Before they could go to the medics, the transport had to pick up several other trainees who were also injured. Their injuries ranged from broken and severely sprained ankles to a broken arm and a concussion. When the transport arrived at the medics' location, John was given a cigarette. As the female medic was about to cut the pants and boots off John, he said, "No, wait," as he took off his boot and dropped his trousers in front of her.

The female medic and several medics laughed because of how brazen John was. No fucks were given, and he didn't want to have to spend the money for new pants or boots. His knee was swollen, and as they did an evaluation on him, one male medic asked John if he was allergic to poultry. Once John replied no, he had his first experience with morphine. The pain was manageable to almost nonexistent as he was transported by ambulance to the military hospital at Fort Benning.

John spent the night at the hospital heavily drugged; his knee was the size of at least two softballs. The military doctor took a needle with a pump attachment and began to pump the fluids out of his knee. After his knee was treated, John was released back to his training class to attend the graduation ceremony the next day. He was still able to graduate jump school since he had successfully completed all five jumps.

With the assistance of crutches, John stood outside the main formation to have his jump wings pinned on his chest. In a process similar to the "pinning" ceremony for a Marine's promotion, one of his black hat instructors stood in front of John with a set of wings in hand, without the backings, placed the wings above his heart, and punched it in. In the Army and Marines, this hazing ritual, known as "blood-winging," occurs when a graduate of jump school receives his jump wings. John would not have it any other way. He was so glad to have his wings pinned deep in his chest. For him it was a rite of passage into the airborne community, even if he was broken and on crutches.

At the conclusion of the graduation ceremony, John was officially jump qualified, although he was concerned about the extent of his injury. He had to drive over nine hours back to Camp Lejeune to be seen by more medical personnel. He would soon learn the future of his career. John had plenty of time to think everything over, and a sense of worry about what might happen next filled his mind. Contemplating all of the things that could or would happen, John accepted the fact that he was severely injured. The extent of it was still unknown, but he would take it step by step and do his best to recover as quickly as possible.

When he arrived home to Amber and Corey, they helped him out of the car, taking his bags inside. When he took his pants off and sat on the couch, his swollen leg was many shades of purple, yellow, black, and blue.

"Daddy, are you hurt?" Corey asked.

"No, buddy. Daddy will be OK; he just had an accident at work," John responded.

"I love you, Daddy!" Corey replied as he gave John a hug.

"I love you too, buddy. I've missed you so much." John held Corey tight.

John went to the Naval Medical Hospital on Camp Lejeune the next day. The doctors informed him that, according to their tests, he had severed all four of his ligaments and torn his meniscus. He would have to have his knee completely reconstructed. However, he would have to wait for the severe swelling to go down before he could get an MRI to confirm the diagnosis. He was placed on limited duty and assigned an administrative position within his CI/HUMINT company. He would have to remain in this position until he fully recovered from his injury and could return to full duty. His future prospects with the Marines were now in jeopardy.

Four months after his midair parachuting accident, John was finally able to have his MRI and knee surgery completed. It was considered an outpatient surgery, and John would be able to recover at home afterward. The doctor replaced all four ligaments with cadaver ligaments and repaired what he could of John's meniscus. When he was recovered enough, John would have to undergo months of intense physical therapy. The doctor informed him that the only thing that had kept his leg together after his accident was his skin. Everything else in his knee was severed and torn. This injury was more serious than he had realized.

After recovering from surgery, John went back to work at his company. Since he remained on light duty, his seat in the CI/HUMINT school was given to another Marine. While still performing his administrative duties, John continued to pursue his bachelor's degree and attend his physical therapy sessions. He was nondeployable and came home from work every day to play with Corey. Although he loved being a father to Corey, he was very unhappy in his marriage to Amber.

Following Corey's birth, John and Amber's sex life was nearly nonexistent. They would have sex once a month to once every six months. John hated the fact that he had to always put in the effort to have sex, while it seemed Amber made no effort at all. Due to the lack of sex, John became indifferent to his wife. Heated arguments and resentment led John to give Amber the same ultimatum again: If she was not going to have sex with him regularly, he was going to continue finding it elsewhere. When an ultimatum is given, it is given from a position of weakness.

"There is no shortage of women that want to have sex with me," he warned for a second time.

Indifferent, Amber said she was fine with that as she was never in the mood to have sex and rarely thought about it. John tried everything from being romantic to helping more around the house to being cold and distant; it seemed there was nothing he could do to change the situation. He felt betrayed and lonely in a marriage he felt stuck in and a "partner" that was more of a roommate than anything.

One day Amber brought up the idea of having a second child so Corey could have a brother or sister. John was already cynical about having another child with a woman who hadn't wanted to have sex with him the last couple years. He didn't want to compound the situation with a new child. But he also thought a second child could strengthen their marriage. Corey would have a sibling, and John would have another child to carry on his last name. Begrudgingly, John agreed to have another child with Amber.

When John agreed, the sex improved immediately. She was all over John every chance she got when he was home. They went from having sex once a month to having sex multiple times a day. Their marriage seemed to improve, and he didn't feel like he was sleeping with a roommate anymore. Then Amber announced that she was pregnant. After this point the sex became less passionate and once again more of a chore for her. The multiple-times-a-day sex dried up to once a day, then once a week, and then back to once a month.

John was so angry with himself for having fallen into such a stupid trap. He felt used, betrayed, and ashamed of himself. The sex had drastically improved not because she desired him more but because it was a means to an end for her. Amber would get what she wanted—another baby. Now instead of one child, they were about to have two children. John felt more stuck in the sexless marriage than he had before. He thought of how much of a fool he had been thinking another child would solve their marital problems. Another child would only compound those problems.

Several months went by with things relatively the same for John. He focused on his work and taking care of Corey. His marriage remained sexless and more of a roommate situation. When Eric was born, John loved him from the moment he saw him, just like he had Corey. Knowing he was stuck in the marriage, John committed himself to being the best father to them. He was going to make sure they grew up to be good, strong men. He was so happy to have another son, although it came at a high cost to him personally. John was giving up a part of himself to stay in an unhappy marriage for the benefit of his sons.

With his family growing, John decided to start house hunting. He wanted to buy a house and move out of the small apartment they were currently living in. John had decided to take some leave for house-hunting purposes when he received a call from his company gunnery sergeant, Gunnery Sergeant Phillips.

"Hey, boss. I know you are on leave, but you need to come into the company office. There is something we need to take care of," he said.

"Well that sounds ominous," John replied.

"We have somethings that we need to take care of right away."

"Roger, Gunny. I'm leaving the house now and should be there in about twenty-five minutes."

As he got dressed, he thought to himself, *What issue needs to be taken care of right away? I took care of all of my work and leave paperwork yesterday.* Still going through a series of questions in his head, he drove onto base and walked into the company building. Gunnery Sergeant Phillips met John in the foyer and asked him to come to his office. *This seems bad*, John thought. *I wonder what is going on right now.*

"Take a seat, John. We have to talk for a moment," Gunnery Sergeant Phillips ordered.

John sat down. "Gunny, what's going on? I don't understand why I got called in here; did I do something wrong?"

"Have you had any problems with your sister, John?" Gunnery Sergeant Phillips asked.

"No, I have a sister and a half sister living with my mother right now, but there haven't been any issues that I'm aware of."

"Well, boss, we have an issue to deal with. There is a warrant out for your arrest, John. There is a sheriff's deputy waiting at the front gate to serve you the warrant and take you into custody. I told him that I would take you to the front gate."

A moment of shock, panic, and questions filled John's mind. *Why is there a warrant for my arrest? I didn't do anything wrong. What's going on; this cannot be happening right now.* "Gunny, I have no idea why there is a warrant out for my arrest. I didn't do anything wrong; I swear to you that I didn't do anything, and this is crazy," John pleaded.

"This is out of my hands. There is nothing I can do right now, and we need to get this over with."

John was in a state of shock. "Roger, Gunny. Let's get this over with."

With that Gunnery Sergeant Phillips drove John to the front gate and met the waiting deputy.

"John Devereaux?" the deputy asked.

"Yes, I'm John."

"I have a warrant for your arrest, and at this time you are under arrest."

As John was handcuffed, his mind flashed back to when he was a police officer and the hundreds of people that he had arrested. He could not believe what was happening. He was innocent of whatever charge they were arresting him for. The ride was quiet as the deputy transported John to the magistrate's office. John remained quiet, although his mind filled with questions and fear over what was going to happen. His freedom, his career, his clearance were all in jeopardy. A sense of hopelessness and worry consumed him.

Standing before the magistrate, John pleaded his innocence, even though any effort to do so was futile. They were going to serve the paperwork regardless. The only chance he had to fight this was in court on his trial date.

"Do you know a Julie Devereaux?" asked the magistrate.

"Yes, she is my half sister, sir," John replied.

"You are being charged with assault on a female, specifically on her. At this time, you are remanded into custody, and I am setting your bond at twenty-five hundred dollars. There is also an emergency protective order against you, and you are to have no contact with her. If you have any weapons or ammunition, you need to turn them over to a responsible individual in accordance with the preliminary protective order."

Still in disbelief about what was happening, John was taken to a holding cell, where for the first time in his life he was the person behind bars. Having been a police officer and having put hundreds of people in jail, he was now the presumed criminal. He continued to wonder why Julie would do this to him. *I have done nothing to her to deserve this*, he thought. Sitting in jail with only his thoughts, he waited for Amber to post his bond and bail him out of jail. Although it was only several hours, it felt like an eternity to John as he was tortured with his thoughts and what-ifs.

After John had been bailed out, he contacted Gunnery Sergeant Phillips and transported his firearms to his house for safekeeping until this was all settled. The gunny knew there was something wrong with this situation. He knew John and his background, that this seemed very out of character for him. Whatever it was, John could rely on him for his support. John and Amber became closer, as she knew John had been wrongfully jailed. Whatever motivations were behind what Julie had done, they would eventually surface.

Because of the unwarranted arrest, Savanah stood up for John against Julie, asking her why she would do something like that. The argument culminated with Linda kicking Savanah and her two children out of the house, since she had sided with Julie. Savanah had nowhere to go and no money to pay for her own place. John told Savanah she and her daughters could move into their two-bedroom apartment temporarily until better accommodations could be made.

It was a tight fit with John, Amber, Corey, and Eric in a two-bedroom apartment. Now there were going to be Savanah and her two daughters, making the small space feel even smaller. John was proud of Savanah for sticking up for him, and he felt that taking her and her daughters in was the right thing to do. He would make sure Savanah and her daughters had a place to stay until the criminal charges were addressed.

Meanwhile John's Top Secret clearance adjudication was suspended pending the outcome of the trial. He continued to work in his normal job and searched for a house to buy, especially since everyone was now living in such tight quarters. One further issue John had to deal with was complications from his first knee reconstruction. The ligaments were failing, and John waited for a second total knee reconstruction. A new baby, criminal charges pending, trying to find a house, a second total knee reconstruction, and his career in jeopardy—it was a stressful time for John.

As he remained in a holding pattern, waiting for everything to work out so he could move on, John did the best he could to stay positive. There was a lot on his plate, and although he was uncertain of what his future might hold, he knew he had to be strong for himself and his family. He was determined not to let Julie ruin his life and career, no matter what. He was ready for this fight, and his attorney was optimistic about the case outcome.

John found and bought the perfect house in a quiet neighborhood close to base. Even with everything still pending, he was confident that he was going to win his case. About two months after moving into his new home, John had his second knee reconstruction. Once again he had all four of his ligaments repaired and recuperated at home on convalescent leave.

A couple weeks later, there was a very bad storm. John heard thunder and saw lightning strike as he sat on the living room couch. The smell of smoke started filling the house. Getting up on his crutches, he saw smoke coming from Eric's bedroom. Eric was asleep in his crib, so he grabbed Eric and on one crutch carried him out of the room. The smoke grew denser. He opened the door to the garage and saw smoke there as well. His house was on fire, so he placed Eric in a baby carrier and took him out of the house. Standing in the rain away from the house, he called the fire department and Amber to notify them the house was on fire. Eric remained covered as John waited for the fire department to arrive.

When the firemen arrived, smoke was clearly emanating from a bedroom and the garage. As the firefighters began to extinguish the fire, Amber arrived, crying and hysterical. John told her to put Eric in the car and wait until the firefighters were done. The fires were quickly put out, and John walked inside to assess the damage. Thankfully, the fires were contained in the room and the garage with no real loss of any personal possessions. It certainly could have been much worse.

This had been the worst year John had experienced in his life. On top of everything else, the house he had just bought had caught on fire during a lightning storm. John thought God was seeking vengeance or testing him for something, and he could not believe so much was happening to him all at the same time.

The house was repaired in short order, better than new. He was recovering from his second surgery, and he was about to attend his trial. He was ready to fight and put this behind him. When the day of the trial arrived, John was nervous and apprehensive about what might happen. If he was convicted, his military career would be over and he would more than likely go to jail and lose his house and family. So much was riding on the outcome of this trial.

As Julie took the stand, she began to speak. "I have to admit something here. John never assaulted me. He did not hit me. I was protecting my boyfriend." Pausing to gather her thoughts. "My boyfriend punched me, and when I went to school, the school resource officer asked who had hit me. I didn't want to get my boyfriend in trouble, so I told him that my brother, John, did it. John never hit me, and I made it up." Her voice was low, and she stared at the ground.

"So why are you just now saying this, Julie?" exclaimed the state's attorney. "Do you understand you falsified a police report? Do you understand what the legal ramifications for that are? Why are you now telling the court this information? Are you lying now or were you lying then?"

"I was trying to protect my boyfriend, but he left me and started seeing another girl. John is innocent; he never touched me."

John's attorney interjected, "Your Honor, in light of this new evidence I am requesting an immediate dismissal of these charges against my client. The 'victim' has perjured herself, and my client has gone through enough emotional damage because of this situation."

"I agree with you, Counselor. In the case of John Devereaux, your charges are dismissed, and you are free to leave," the judge responded.

A huge sense of relief swept over John. For months he had been waiting for clear vindication that he had done nothing wrong—having spent thousands of dollars for an attorney and to be bailed out of jail for a crime he did not commit. Although his relationships with Julie and Linda were forever broken, this dismissal allowed John to finally move on with his life. Crutching himself out of the courtroom, John called Gunnery Sergeant Phillips and informed him of what had happened. Somehow Gunnery

Sergeant Phillips was not surprised. He had seen several Marines be wrongly jailed and lose their careers due to false allegations.

After the trial John returned to work. His security clearance was favorably adjudicated shortly afterward. His sister Savanah and her two daughters moved into a place of their own. John learned later on that to avoid charges, Julie had quit high school a month before graduation. She and Linda had moved back to upstate New York, their fates forever unknown. After what Julie had done to him, he could never and would never forgive her. There was no trust, and, in his opinion, she was no longer his half sister but a liability.

Not only had John not known his biological father but he had also lost his stepfather to another woman and lost his mother and his half sister to lies and deceit. Even during the trial process, he had been considered guilty by his grandparents. John proudly walked away from all of them. His only remaining family were Savanah and her two daughters (whom he was not very close with), Amber, and his two sons, Corey and Eric. He was fine with that because his sons were the most important part of his life.

Although it had been a hellacious year for John, he was able to move on, and life seemed somewhat normal. Due to his second knee reconstruction, John was automatically placed on a physical evaluation board (PEB), where it would be determined whether he was physically cable of remaining in the Marines. Although John tried to be optimistic, he knew what the outcome was going to be. His seat at the CI/HUMINT school was gone, yet he remained working at the company until his results came back.

The PEB process takes a substantial amount of time in cases where medical separation of a service member is under consideration. A year and a half after his first surgery and several months after his second surgery, he received the news. He was going to be medically separated under honorable conditions. His future aspirations of becoming a Marine officer were gone in an instant—he had suspected this was going to be the case when his riser had snapped his knee. Thankfully, he would be leaving the Marines with a Top Secret clearance and was only months away from completing his bachelor's degree.

Several days after Christmas, John was officially separated from the Marines. Due to the nature of the injury he had incurred in the line of duty, which was considered combat related, John was given a modest severance package. He was able to collect his VA benefits in conjunction with his severance. Had this not been a combat-related injury, John would have had to hand the severance money over to the VA. Or he would have had to wait until it was paid off before the VA would provide him with his monthly disability check. In this instance John was fortunate enough to collect both; the VA disability check he would be able to collect for life.

Once separated from the Marines, John continued working on his degree while also being a stay-at-home dad for Eric and applying to any jobs within the intelligence community. His Top Secret clearance was invaluable for starting a cleared intel career. Many government contract companies require you to already have your clearance. Most companies don't want to spend the thousands upon thousands of dollars to sponsor someone through the process.

For four months John applied to job after job. Arguments between John and Amber continued because she would take his severance money and go on shopping sprees. John had to explain to her that that was the only income he had right now aside from the VA disability checks. Until he got a job, they needed to be careful about money. Amber was never good at managing money, which caused a lot of arguments. A couple months after separation, John received a phone call regarding a position down in Florida, working for the government as a defense contractor.

The pay offered was excellent, and it kept him within the intelligence community. Although he could not be an active-duty Marine anymore, he was getting closer to his goal of working for the CIA. By staying in the intelligence community and keeping his clearance, he still had a shot. After a short discussion with Amber, John explained he was taking the position and began to plan his move down to Florida, the location of which also happened to be about two towns away from Amber's family. To John this new career was a godsend, and he was very excited to move and explore this new opportunity.

CHAPTER 8

John listed his house in North Carolina. Amber and his sons would remain in North Carolina until the house sold, while John would live with Amber's family temporarily. Once the house sold, he would rent a home so they could start another new chapter of their lives in Florida. Although he was going to be living with her family, John was excited to have some sense of independence from Amber. Their marriage was under constant strain; they had even undergone marriage counseling in North Carolina.

Once his vehicle was packed, John kissed Corey and Eric and told them that he would see them soon enough. He briefly kissed Amber before getting into his car and beginning the long drive to Destin, Florida. During his trip, he thought often about his sons and hoped that he would get to see them soon. He thought about his hope that the house would sell quickly. And the first inkling of wanting a divorce from Amber began to set in. He was tired of being in a sexless, loveless marriage to a narcissistic woman who only valued herself, not her husband

and children. He was tired of her irrational mood swings and the drama that often followed them.

He began formulating a plan to strategically divorce Amber. The only reason John had remained married to her was the children. He didn't want another man to raise his sons. He knew of the many stories of men who got divorced and never got to see their children again, having to pay large sums in child support while the mothers brought random men home. John didn't want that for his sons, but he could not stand to be married to Amber for much longer.

John reasoned that a move to Florida was the perfect opportunity to set his plan in motion. She would be near her family support network in case she needed anything. His sons would have a steady family to help them if he could not be in their lives, but he was going to make every effort to keep them in his life. John knew he had married the wrong woman, and it was time for his exit. Additionally, his new career in Florida would be stable, and he would remain in the area to stay close to his sons. John was becoming more resolute about his plan and what he had to do.

Arriving in the early morning hours at Amber's parents' home, John was greeted with hugs and settled into his new room. He had the weekend to get his affairs in order before starting his new job on Monday. There was already a sense of peace in freedom enveloping John as he began unpacking his things. Although this was going to be a temporary situation, Amber's family loved having John stay with them. He was loved and respected by everyone in her family, even if not by Amber herself.

Enjoying the beautiful weather, John went to the beach. He had never seen such beautiful white-sand beaches and crystal-clear, teal-blue water in his life. It was like an image out of a postcard or travel magazine. Lying on the beach, his eyes gazing upon the water, an ice-cold beer next to him, he relaxed as pretty women in string bikinis sunbathed or went for a dip in the ocean. Families and children played in the sand and water. John was so at ease; a sense of peace overcame him. He had not felt this level of peace in a very long time, and he didn't want it to end.

CONTRACTING FOR THE GOVERNMENT

Like all great and relaxing weekends, that one went by too quickly. Next thing he knew, it was Monday morning, and he had to report to his first day on the job. He would be working as an intelligence analyst for Air Force Special Operations Command (AFSOC) at Hurlburt Field, a small special operations base. When he arrived at the base, he was greeted by his new manager, who advised John that he would be working in the 11th Special Operations Intelligence Squadron (SOIS). There John would be involved in the process of providing tailored unmanned aerial vehicle (UAV) full-motion video processing, exploitation, and dissemination (PED) for special operations forces engaged in both combat and noncombat operations worldwide.

Although John was no longer in the military, this civilian contract kept John involved in the military and intelligence communities. He would still be able to have an impact on secret operations all over the world. For him this was a step up from his days in the infantry and special operations and his tenure as a police officer. This position also had the potential for exponential career growth and development. Plus, he loved his new salary, as he was making more money than he ever had before. With a promising career and great salary, John no longer wanted the burden or liability of being tied down to Amber.

After completing his initial training, John reported to C flight as his permanent duty assignment. He worked twelve-hour shifts with an alternating day- and night-shift schedule every three months. Although the hours being inside one building staring at screens the whole time felt long, he also had ample time off from his schedule to recharge and relax. So far everything was working out perfectly, and John was very happy. He even liked his immediate supervisor, Dominic "Dom" Faruzzi. Dom was retired from the US Air Force, a world-class supervisor and mentor. John and Dom quickly became great friends, both knowing the boundaries between supervisor and employee.

That first month John genuinely enjoyed the work he was doing. He completed his bachelor's degree in criminal justice with a specialization in homeland security cum laude, his house in North Carolina sold, and he was about to be with his sons. The only thing he was not happy about was the fact that Amber was going to be coming down. The freedom he had had in her absence was going to be taken away. *This is all part of the plan*, John reasoned with himself. Inevitably he would have to live and deal with her for a short time before he could execute his plan.

John found a home to rent in the very large subdivision Holley by the Sea, located in Navarre, Florida, approximately thirty minutes from work. John signed the lease for a year. One year was his time frame to plan and execute his exit strategy. When Amber and his sons arrived, they moved their belongings into the new home. John was so happy to see his sons, and they were equally happy to see him. He loved his sons with all his heart and mind.

Almost immediately after moving back in together, Amber and John began arguing. She was unable to find a decent-paying job and took her frustrations out on John, even accusing him of cheating with coworkers because he had such a weird schedule. John thought that in reality she was deflecting and projecting her problems onto him. Instead of paying any mind to her or what she was accusing him of, John focused on himself. He knew that he wanted to complete his master's degree, a feat nobody in his family had ever achieved. He also realized he needed to get back into shape and, most importantly, quit smoking.

John's career at the 11th was going well. Working as a multisource analyst (MSA), he became an instructor for new MSAs on his flight. Eventually he added another qualification to his résumé, full-motion video (FMV) analyst. In this position John would stare at a screen for a period of time, never taking his eyes away and calling out any and all activity he detected. During periods of inactivity, those felt like very long nights, especially at 2:00 a.m.—trying to stay awake and focused, only to come home to a nagging wife.

One day at work, out of nowhere, a sharp pain began emanating from John's kneecap as he tried to straighten his leg. He could barely move his leg without excruciating pain. He advised Dom that he had to go to the hospital. His leg was in such pain, he needed two coworkers to walk him to his truck. While in the truck, seated in an awkward position, John drove himself to the hospital. He notified Amber of what was happening and asked her to meet him at the hospital.

The ER staff seemed indifferent to what John was reporting. He sat in the waiting room for over an hour; Amber arrived as John was finally escorted to a room to be seen by a doctor. After an initial, painful evaluation, the doctor ordered X-rays. As soon as the X-rays came back, the doctor and several nurses came into the room. The doctor administered morphine and advised him that a screw previously drilled into his femur from the second knee reconstruction had come out and lodged in his knee. That's why he could not extend his leg.

They were unable to do immediate surgery, so John had to wait a long and painful week for the screw to be removed. When the surgery was finally completed, John was able to straighten his leg. The doctor removed excessive scar tissue and the titanium screw. Although he didn't have to have physical therapy, John was relieved it was over and he could focus on getting his knee and legs stronger. Because it was an outpatient and not very invasive surgery, John was able to recover and resume his duties at work.

A month after surgery, John had pretty much fully recovered. He could now walk up steps with no difficulty, something he had not been able to do since his second knee surgery. He felt like he had been given a second lease on life, and he wasn't going to waste it. Now was the time to put his plan into motion. After work John would go on long walks. Those walks turned into jogging and then into running. Although he only ran a mile or two, this was the first time in over three years he had been able to run. John even joined a local CrossFit gym with his coworker and friend Chris. Slowly John was getting back into pre–parachuting accident shape.

The one thing that was slowing him down was his eleven-year pack-and-a-half-a-day smoking habit. He could feel how constricted his lungs were as he worked out and ran. For his health and to increase his physical endurance, John dropped the cigarettes. The first two weeks were the toughest. His body was so accustomed to nicotine; he used the nicotine patch for three days before deciding he needed to embrace the withdrawals instead of fighting them. He had done this to his body, and this was his body repairing itself. When he learned to enjoy the cravings, quitting smoking became so much easier.

Amber noticed a change in John once he quit smoking and started exercising and working on his master's degree, though she didn't know its precise nature. They were seeing a marriage counselor in Florida because their issues had not been resolved. John had checked out of the marriage a long time ago, and he was just going through the motions, preparing himself for the imminent divorce.

As he sat alone in the garage, in a 1974 Dodge Charger two years into a full body restoration, Amber opened the door and asked him what he was doing.

"I'm just sitting here looking at my project." A momentary pause. "Are you in love with me?" he asked Amber quizzically.

"I love you, John, but I'm not in love with you," she responded.

John thought to himself, *This marriage is over. I'm no longer wasting my time and freedom. I'm still going to be the best father I can to my kids. I'm done with her shit, and I'm moving on.*

"I want a divorce," John replied calmly.

In near disbelief she said, "Fine."

The next day they attended their marriage counseling appointment. John advised the counselor that he had told Amber he wanted a divorce. He also told her nothing was going to change his mind. He was done and wanted out of the marriage—no chance of reconciliation, no forgiveness, no more tries. For nine and a half years, he had despised Amber, and he was through. Knowing nothing would change his resolve, John felt a euphoria of emotions. He felt like he was no longer in prison and focused on his upcoming freedom.

Just the possibilities of a single life were enough to reinforce his thoughts. He was making the right decision for himself. The divorce itself was not as "messy" as the ones some of his friends and coworkers had endured. Initially Amber requested over $2,500 in child support and alimony as well.

John retorted, "I am not paying that absurd amount of money. I will stay 'married' to you and still fuck whomever I want and do whatever I want. Your best option is to move on with your life like I have. We can make this a clean break, or I can make this drag out indefinitely."

Amber agreed to move on; she saw there was no turning back. The divorce was going to happen whether she liked it or not. This made for an uncomfortable living arrangement. John slept in a spare bedroom, while Amber remained in the master bedroom. Amber even went as far as attempting to seduce John into having sex with her again. She was repeatedly shut down; John was disgusted by her, and he was no longer remotely attracted to her. Realizing sex with her was no longer of value to John, she capitulated and accepted the situation for what it was. She knew he was not going to change his mind.

The separation was addressed. John and Amber agreed to the terms of custody, living accommodations, child support, Corey's and Eric's schools, the division of property and assets. Everything was officially in writing through their attorney; all they had to do was wait for the court's final dissolution of marriage.

Officially separated, John and Amber began living in their respective apartments. John returned to the single life for the first time since leaving the Marines. He felt like he had his life back. Even though he had joint custody of his children, John had more time to devote to work, school, and the gym. He was making impressive gains and started to compete in triathlons. John had not been this happy in a very long time.

Occasionally, Amber would ask him for more money. Even though he was already paying her $1,500 a month in child support, it never seemed to be enough for her. For his kids' sake, he would help her out.

John's career was also going very well. He qualified for a third coveted position—that of screener. The screener supervised the PED. When the FMVs made a call out, he would provide the information to forward deployed units. The screener was also the one point of contact between the UAV aircrew; the Intelligence, Surveillance, and Reconnaissance Tactical Controller (ITC); and the PED of four people.

It was a big step up from his beginnings as an MSA. At work John would talk with Dom and Chris about the divorce, and they would always offer great advice. He knew he could always turn to them if he needed help, and vice versa. They knew divorces were never easy, as they had seen nasty ones in their careers.

This was John's life for the summer and leading into the fall—working and working out while waiting for the finalization of his divorce from Amber. On his days off, John would see his sons, who were vocal about being sad he was not living with them. They appeared to be adapting to the new situation. Although it was not a perfect arrangement, John was there for his sons no matter what. He was dismayed to see that Corey's grades were beginning to suffer, that his son had turned into a C student.

At the end of October 2012, John received the finalized divorce paperwork. Nine and a half years of marriage were finally dissolved, and he was legally free from Amber. Trying to date, John had met a couple women through his gym and at work. Having just gotten out of a long, terrible marriage, John was not ready for anything serious. He was done with relationships for the time being.

John attended mandatory work training a month after finalizing his divorce. There he encountered two new hires attending the basic analyst course. One of the new hires was a petite blond woman who was mildly attractive; the other, however, immediately caught his eye.

With short brown hair, black glasses, and a light-purple pashmina wrapped around her, she had an air of intelligence and sophistication akin to that of a serious student. His brain told him, *This is her; this is the "one" that I am going to be with.* He didn't question this feeling because he had never felt a feeling like this before. As if in a Hollywood love story, he thought to himself, *This is it, this is what love at first sight is.*

He didn't approach her other than to say a casual hello; he didn't know her name, where she was from, or anything about her for that matter. He knew there was an immediate attraction and that he was going to be with her. It was like a voice inside his head and heart understood something that he could not quantifiably explain. It was a sense, a feeling, a desire for a complete stranger that seemed so unreasonable but felt so right. Whatever it was he was feeling, he was going to find out all about her and make her his. Any lingering doubts about leaving Amber were gone. He was consumed by and infatuated with this beautiful woman.

Coming into work one day, he was surprised to see both new hires on his flight. They were going to be working as MSAs, and John was going to be training the woman he was infatuated with. *It is fate that she would end up on my flight, and I would be her trainer,* thought John.

John approached his new trainee with confidence. "Hi, I'm John, and I'm going to be your MSA trainer."

With a warm smile, she responded, "Hi, John. I'm Davina, Davina Anderson."

"It's nice to meet you; let's get started with your training," John replied coolly.

As they began training, they had casual conversations, learning about each other, John sensing a sexual tension. He was sure she felt the same, although he kept things professional, as he didn't want any work-related issues to complicate his career.

As the weeks passed, John and Davina continued to converse. John found out she had a long-distance boyfriend in Maryland, though he also learned that he and Davina had many similar and complementary hobbies. The attraction between them was very apparent. Even other coworkers saw the sexual tension and attraction between them. Side comments were made by coworkers, who said they looked like a great couple and matched perfectly. The only thing in the way of their being together was the long-distance boyfriend.

Hanging out one night watching a movie at John's apartment, John and Davina touched hands for the first time. As Davina lay on her back on his couch, John on top her, he went to kiss her on the lips.

"I have a boyfriend, and although I'm very attracted to you, I can't kiss you until I end my relationship with him," she said.

"I totally understand," John replied as he backed off her.

"It's getting late, and if I stay here, I might do something I regret," Davina stated as she stood from the couch.

Before leaving, Davina let out a soft moan as John kissed her neck.

"I look forward to seeing you tomorrow," said John.

"As do I," Davina responded before leaving his apartment and heading to hers.

The next morning John received a call from Davina. "Hey, John, would you like to come over to my apartment?"

"Yeah, sure, I'll be over there in a little bit."

Within thirty minutes John was knocking on Davina's apartment door. She opened the door, smiled at him, and told him to come inside.

"I broke up with my boyfriend last night; I want to be with you."

"I want to be with you too. I have wanted you since the moment I laid eyes on you."

As they edged closer together, John grabbed Davina and went in for a kiss. They embraced, hands feeling and exploring each other's bodies for the very first time. Both of their hands were shaking from nervousness. Within mere hours of Davina breaking up with her long-distance boyfriend, John and Davina were having passionate sex. All of the pent-up sexual tension was released. John was addicted, the seeming Hollywood fantasy having come true in real life.

They slept in each other's arms for the remainder of the afternoon. John deeply kissed Davina before heading to his apartment to shower and change in anticipation of work that night. During the night shift, John and Davina smiled, their eyes connecting in the knowledge of how intimate they had been only a few hours before. The sexual tension was still present as they stood next to each other during the prework briefing.

This relationship was the romance John had always pictured. He had found his "one," his "soul mate" in Davina. Everything he felt for Davina was the opposite of whatever he had felt about Amber. Everything seemed perfect; friends and coworkers commented that theirs was the sort of model romance to which everyone aspires. Their relationship went from zero to sixty in a matter of weeks. Davina spent all her time in John's apartment. They ultimately decided to move in together when their leases expired.

Six months into their relationship, John and Davina ended their leases and rented a single-family home in Holley by the Sea. John's sons had taken an immediate liking to Davina and loved being around her. John thought that this was too good to be true—after all this time, he was going to have the family he had always wanted. Since Davina didn't want children, John's having two sons seemed to be a complementary fit that would work for everyone. The kids would have a loving stepparent, and John would have a soon-to-be wife and loving partner.

Although their schedules were difficult with rotating days and night shifts, their relationship wasn't an issue in the workplace. In fact it allowed them to spend more time together. Coworkers gave them the nickname "Davren," apparently the type of name given to power couples in Hollywood. It was an affectionate term both John and Davina accepted freely. With everything going so well for them, the only thing John still wanted was for his sons to live with him full time so he could have his family all together.

Shortly after Christmas 2013, John's dream came true. Amber asked John if he could take the boys full time. She claimed she could not afford to take care of them, even with the $1,500 a month in child support she received from John. Without hesitation, and with Davina's blessing, John immediately said yes and moved Corey and Eric into the house that night. His dream was being realized; his family was together. With his old school way of thinking, John wanted Davina as his wife. Although she was opposed to being married again, John assumed that with time she would change her mind.

John accepted Davina for who she was as a person, her tattoos and piercings, her changing hairstyle and hair color. He had placed her on a pedestal, and he would do everything he could to make sure she was happy. He was deeply in love and infatuated with Davina; he didn't want a life without her in it. Internally, though, he had this nagging feeling that this relationship was not going to last forever.

It's only in my mind, John reasoned. *Everything is going so well; we will make this work no matter what.*

The addition of Corey and Eric brought challenges to John and Davina's home and work relationships. Initially, John and Davina worked the same day/night twelve-hour rotating shift. Every three months they would rotate from day shift to night shift and then from night shift to day shift. All of that changed when the boys came to live with John and Davina. To ensure a parent was home when the boys were, John and Davina alternated their work schedules. When John worked the day shift, Davina worked the night shift. They really only saw each other at shift change or on their days off. Although the new work schedules and introduction of the boys into their lives presented challenges, John saw this as a way to strengthen their relationship and overcome any obstacles. They were meant to be, he remained convinced.

As the government contract was being disputed at work, contractors were facing possible layoffs. With the stress of losing their jobs, the children at home, alternating schedules, studying for their respective master's degree programs, and Amber's incessant attempts to insinuate herself in their lives, the relationship between John and Davina was becoming strained. The relationship was not what it had been in the beginning, although this was not outwardly acknowledged. Their sex life remained consistent, something John was not accustomed to because of Amber, but John knew it was time to move and find more secure jobs in a different area.

Their job search began in Florida at first, as they wanted to remain in the state. They also wanted to be able to work for the same company in the same area. This would allow them to take care of the boys. The search proved to be very difficult. With no return calls on submitted résumés, John and Davina started to apply for jobs outside of Florida, but still with no luck. As contractors continued to be laid off, they wondered when it was going to be their turn.

Although John received a steady government disability check, he was worried that he would lose his job and be unable to support his family. One way or another, he was going to make it work. But in that moment, he didn't have a plan beyond continuing to submit résumé after résumé.

In the summer of 2014, John and Davina received a call from a large government contracting business located within the Northern Virginia and DC area seeking the skills they possessed. John saw this as an excellent opportunity. He had just completed his master's degree in intelligence studies with honors, and Davina was continuing to work on her master's program. The starting salary was nearly double what they were making in Florida. They decided that this was an opportunity they could not pass up. This was going to be a steady, essential career that would not have the instability of other government contracts.

John and Davina began planning a move from Florida to the DC area. Corey and Eric were very adaptable, so John and Davina were not worried about them changing homes. John made sure the boys would be raised in a safe neighborhood, since the DC area was synonymous with crime. Before making such a major move, John and Davina came up with a list of homes they were interested in purchasing. Housing in Northern Virginia was incredibly expensive, nearly double the cost of Florida homes.

John planned to fly up to Northern Virginia for one day. He would meet their Realtor and look at each of the homes on their list. Since John had already remodeled a couple homes, and due to his combined military and police background, he knew what to look for in a neighborhood. There wasn't a lot of time to waste in his home search. Davina trusted him to make the best choice for her and the boys. And so the search began as the Realtor picked him up from the airport.

Many of the homes were from the mid-1970s and needed a lot of work. Finding a modern, updated home close to their new workplace was out of the question. The market was just too expensive. Davina had received a preapproved home loan because she wanted to buy her first home. With the financial parameters set, John made sure they remained within her budget.

Although it was not easy, he did find the perfect home in Sterling, Virginia. It was older but had a lot of potential. It matched their prerequisite of being in a good, safe location. The school district was excellent, and schools were within walking distance of the house, which was located on a cul-de-sac only thirty-five minutes from work by car.

Having found their ideal future home, John and Davina submitted an offer. There was no time to waste. They were projected to move to Northern Virginia at the end of October. With a home offer accepted and their start dates secured, John and Davina prepared for their move. Although Amber attempted to stop John from taking the boys to another state, they came up with a contractual agreement to appease Amber. That said, she only saw the boys three times over a period of a year, despite John's expressed desire that she spend more time with them.

MOVING TO NORTHERN VIRGINIA

John and his family moved to Northern Virginia and stayed in a hotel for a week until the closing paperwork was completed. Although, during the last year, their relationship had endured a lot of stress and some hardships, John and Davina were going to start a new chapter in their lives with a new home and career in a new state, further separating them from Amber's attempted intrusions into their lives. Despite the bumps, the relationship was stronger than ever in John's mind. Davina never wanted for or needed anything, and they were soon going to be living the American dream.

The stress of moving passed. They settled into their new home and careers. The boys were in new schools and adapting well; life was going to plan. Even the new schedule of working a month of days followed by a rotation of a month of nights didn't have an apparent impact on their relationship. They had endured that schedule in Florida and made it work. Being on different shifts gave them separation at work. They were able to spend their days off with each other, even though they were on opposite schedules, which led to sleep deprivation.

John participated in numerous marathons and Ironman triathlon racing events in the first six months after their move, despite his busy work schedule. At times they did these races as a family. John was ready to propose. He wanted Davina to be his wife and stepmother to his sons. They were already calling her mom and loved her very much. Being old fashioned and wanting a steady, traditional family unit, John took Davina to Tiffany's in Tysons Corner, Virginia. There she could pick out the exact the ring she wanted. He did this knowing that Davina was more progressive than he; John wanted her to have an engagement ring of her choosing.

While sitting on a bench in their backyard during a warm summer day, John professed his love to Davina. She accepted John's proposal. They were now engaged, and he was ready to spend the rest of his life with her, even as he still sensed this relationship was not going to last. Going forward, their friends were happy, and from all outward appearances John and Davina were happy. Everything was on track for a long and wonderful future.

As they discussed wedding plans, Davina told John that she didn't want to change her last name to his and she still did not want to have children. Davina's desire not to change her name became a sticking point for John and resulted in the biggest argument they had had up to that point. He explained to Davina that taking his last name was something extremely important to him, yet she was adamant about keeping her last name.

The argument was intense. They both discussed moving on and breaking up since they could not reach a compromise. Sitting at a local Starbucks, they discussed future plans with and without each other. Yet, not wanting to lose Davina over something that was trivial from her point of view and still thinking of her as on a pedestal, John acquiesced. He accepted the hyphenation of their last names as a compromise, although he took this as an insult from a woman claiming she wanted to share the rest of her life with him and the boys.

The argument changed the relationship dynamic from John's perspective. Everything seemed different from that point forward. Although he was engaged to Davina, John was not as successful in his new career as Davina was in hers. The boys and Amber were a source of constant stress. A little over a month after their major argument, John found out Amber was seriously dating a three-time convicted felon. Not wanting his sons to be exposed to such a violent criminal, he advised Amber that the boys were not going to see her down there unless her new man agreed to have no contact with them.

This caused a firestorm of legal action as Amber took John to court. John flew down to Florida to fight for his sons. His goal was for his boys not to have any interaction with Amber's boyfriend (he later found out in the hearing that this man was in fact her new husband). The court sided with John and agreed that Amber had displayed a serious lack of judgment in marrying this man. John was awarded full custody of Corey and Eric with very specific visitation rights for Amber. During the hearing, Amber made every conceivable allegation to discredit John as a father, even when there was no evidential proof.

The court agreed with John's defense and concerns. Having claimed victory, John left Florida with the legal documentation that would allow him to keep his sons with him. Although John was able to keep his sons, this further strained the relationship between John and Davina. There was always a source of stress in their lives, which wore John and Davina down. It was exhausting working the rotating schedule, constantly having to deal with Amber and her attempts at legal action. John could sense Davina distancing herself from him, although she never explicitly discussed what was on her mind.

John started to drink more as the stressors of life began to get to him. He would find the escape and re-laxation he desperately needed in the bottle. Although he loved his sons dearly, life was becoming too much for John. He was no longer finding pleasure in training for races or his career. He was falling into a dark place from which there seemed to be no escape. This was furthered when John decided to shave his receding hairline and sport the bald look. He was planning to have a hair transplant, but the constant attorney fees and bills prevented his saving enough to pay for the procedure. John's training began to suffer as he sank further into depression and began to steadily gain weight.

John gained over twenty-five pounds and was constantly angry at the world around him. Nothing ever seemed to be going the way he wanted it to. There was always a challenge or stressor without end. If it was not one thing, it was another. He hated the way he looked and felt. The internalized moral guilt of participating in the deaths of nearly five hundred people for his work only exacerbated his self-loathing. He was living in a hell. John devoutly loved Davina and his sons, but it seemed everything else kept intentionally getting in the way.

CHAPTER 9

I n the spring of 2016, John and Davina's careers hit a high note. They both received a coveted addition to their Top Secret clearances by passing a lifestyle polygraph. This was known as the "golden ticket" and made John and Davina even more marketable, especially with their military, intelligence, and education backgrounds. With this new clearance level, John and Davina were able to leave their current program and enjoy a normal, consistent schedule while working in a higher-status career. Having worked nearly five years on a rotating shift schedule, John was elated to have some semblance of a normal life.

This new opportunity also provided John and Davina a solution to the constant issue of finding day care. With this new schedule, it would also make day care easier, since the boys would be in school while they were at work. Not to mention their new careers brought about a significant pay increase. Although they had been doing well since moving up from Florida, their promotions allowed them to be financially comfortable, something

John hadn't experienced in the years since his marriage to Amber.

John continued to run and do triathlon and half-Ironman races. The next big race was the Ironman Lake Placid triathlon. For over a year, John trained on his days off for the grueling 2.4-mile swim, 112-mile bike ride, and 26.2-mile marathon, the events to be completed back-to-back and within prescribed time periods. This was something John had thought nearly impossible since his parachuting accident. But he was determined to start and finish that race and thus earn the tittle "Ironman." He was focused and driven to succeed as the Ironman race consumed his thoughts daily.

In late July, with everything packed and his gear ready to go, John, Davina, and the boys drove up to Lake Placid for the Ironman event. Having grown up a few hours' drive from Lake Placid, John was filled with a sense of nostalgia. He hadn't been this far north in the Adirondack Mountains in over ten years. The only reason he had returned was to compete in this event. He still had had no contact with his mother or stepsister in the nearly seven years since his arrest and had no intention in changing that.

In the chilly early morning hours, triathletes were preparing their gear for the race, which was only a few hours away; they were ensuring that their bikes had the proper tire pressure, that nutrition was ready to go, and that all of their gear was perfectly staged in anticipation of the transition between events. This was going to be a grueling 140.6-mile race that would test the heart and drive of every participant. Some were world-class athletes driven to finish first, while others, like John, wanted to finish this race and earn the Ironman title. All of his training; previous races used to hone his body, mind, and equipment; and hours spent away from Davina and the boys had led up to this one race.

Once the national anthem had been played and the announcer had finished speaking, John began counting down the seconds before the start of the race; he kissed Davina and told her that he loved her before joining the group of triathletes. With a loud gunshot, the 2.4-mile swim event began. John actively disliked the swim portion of triathlon. Countless times during the swim portion of previous races, he had become entangled with other athletes, sometimes getting kicked in the face or having his goggles knocked off; this was going to be the longest distance swim of his life. Thankfully, the water was crystal clear, which had not been the case in previous races.

John entered the cold water, which was chilly even though he was wearing a wet suit. The water took his breath away, causing his heart to beat fast. *Relax and gain control of your breathing*, he said to himself. He was focused solely on the swim. He didn't have time to think about the other events. He needed to finish this event first. After his first lap, he only had one lap remaining. Many of the faster swimmers had already transitioned to the bike portion as he began his second lap. With less people in the water, it was much easier for John to stay focused without having to fight for swim space.

John emerged from the water an hour and a half from when he had first entered the water. He couldn't believe he had swum 2.4 miles. This gave him a surge of energy and motivation for the next event, the 112-mile bike through the Adirondacks. Although the bike corral was mostly empty, he transitioned from the swim and quickly put on his bike gear. It was a race against the clock, and although he felt like he had fallen behind, he knew he had to pace himself. He had seen it all too often—athletes going all in at the beginning only to burn themselves out at the end.

John knew he would make up a lot of ground on the bike, especially since the biking event was taking place in the mountains. Each mile he went was one mile closer to the next event. For over seven and a half hours, Breaking Benjamin's "I Will Not Bow" and the Script's "Hall of Fame" replayed in his head over and over. His legs exhausted from biking, he tried not to focus on the pain and thought of Davina and his sons. He was not going to fail in front of them; he was not going to fail himself. With a very sore ass and cramped, weak legs, John rode into the bike transition, having completed the bike portion of the race in just over seven and a half hours and now nine hours into the race.

As he ran into the marathon transition tent, John realized he had eight hours left to complete the marathon in order to finish the race within the allotted time. If he failed to make the 26.2-mile run in that time, everything he had done up to that point would have been wasted. Digging deep in himself, he started the final portion of the race. The only thing between him and becoming an Ironman was a few miles.

During the marathon portion of the event, spectators and family members cheered their loved ones, giving them surges of energy, even if only for a moment. When John finished the first 13.1-mile lap, he kissed Davina and the boys, telling them he loved them before heading out on his second lap. The smiles on his sons' faces, telling him he could do it, were very powerful for John. The second lap seemed to take an eternity. Alternating between running and walking due to the severe cramps in his legs, he was hell bent on making it to the finish line. He set distances to run and distances to walk, pushing himself harder each time.

Fifteen and a half hours into the race, John crossed the finish line. The announcer proclaimed the words he had trained so hard for over the last few years: "John Devereaux, you are an Ironman!" John had accomplished his goal of finishing an Ironman race, even with his leg still messed up from the midair parachuting accident just over eight years ago. He hugged his family tight when they met him at the finish line. He had done it; everything he had sacrificed and trained for had culminated in this moment of being an Ironman—like "Marine," a title no person can take away.

A week later, as John finished up work, he messaged Davina to tell her he was heading home.

"I love you," he wrote at the end of their conversation.

"I love you too," she replied.

What John didn't realize was that in two hours, everything—his whole life—would be different.

Sitting outside after learning Davina didn't want to be with him anymore, John felt as if his heart had been torn open. He should have been used to this since everyone except his sons had left him in some way or another. He was used to pain, but this was something he had never felt before. Davina and his sons were truly the best things that had ever happened to him.

With Davina having given no explanation other than that she was not in love with him and didn't want to be a stepmother, John grasped for answers. He knew things had been a little rocky in the months leading up the Ironman race, but he thought they had settled their problems. When questioned, Davina held firm, her heart and eyes cold as ice. This was not the woman he had supposedly known for three and a half years. He was staring at a complete stranger who had suddenly flipped a light switch from a warm, loving heart to a cold and callous one. He could not believe what was happening. The love of his life, his soul mate, was leaving him and the boys.

As Davina walked back into the house to retrieve her things (she planned to stay at a friend's), Eric stood on the stairs with his arms open. With tears in his eyes, he pleaded, "Mommy, please don't leave me."

"Get out of my way," she responded as she moved past him, completely unsympathetic to the crying seven-year-old boy.

Corey, who was only eleven years old at the time, cried on the couch. They were losing their "mom" and didn't know why. Corey pleaded with John, "Please, Daddy, I will do anything for her to stay; I'll be a good boy, and I won't cause any more problems."

John held Corey tight and told him that it was not his fault and that he loved him so much. "It's her decision to leave, and you have done nothing wrong. Davina doesn't want to be with us anymore, and there is nothing we can do to stop that."

A few minutes later, Davina emerged from the bedroom with a suitcase and handbag packed with her things. As she walked out the door, John pleaded, "It's not too late to turn this around; we can still work this out."

"I don't love you, John, and this whole situation does not feel right," she exclaimed before walking out the door.

Once the door shut, John's heart was more broken than it had ever been. He also knew he needed to comfort the boys first. He would have plenty of time later, after the boys were in bed, to think about what had happened that day.

A few hours later, John sat on the couch, reflecting on Davina's actions. He could not understand how a woman who had once wanted to spend the rest of her life with him and the boys could walk out so heartlessly. There had been no emotion in her when she left, and John tried to logically come up with a reason as to why.

He was flooded with memories of their past vacations. The great times they had shared and adversities they had overcome. John was longing for Davina to come back home. He had known this day was going to come. *Nothing good in my life never remains,* he thought. As he sat outside with a loaded gun in his hand, tears began to fill his eyes. He recalled the first time he had held a gun to his head; this time his whole world seemed to crash down on him like a ton of bricks. He was mentally in a very dark place, and he saw no other option but to end the pain. He could not and did not want to see a life without her. John had given her everything. Although he was not a perfect person, he thought he had been a good man to her.

She was his world, and now his world was gone, and no matter what he tried to say or do, there was no getting her back. All of the Hollywood movies he had watched where they guy got the girl back were just fairy-tale illusions. Gripping the handgun, his finger resting on the trigger as tears filled his eyes—all it would take was one gentle squeeze of the trigger, and all he ever was would be gone. The shell of a man who has lived a life of only pain and violence.

Taking deep breaths, John tried to find the courage in himself to pull the trigger. He wanted to end the misery as he rested the barrel on his right temple. His hands shaking, flush and filled with what seemed like insurmountable pain, he thought, *This is how it ends.* The years of war, witnessing the violence on the street, being responsible for the killing of nearly five hundred terrorists across the world while working for the government, and losing the one woman he could not bear to lose—the pain must end here and now.

He was resolute, determined to pull the trigger. This was going to happen. John wasn't thinking about the future or his two young sons sleeping upstairs, who would lose a father. John could only think of himself and the pain he felt. As he was about to pull the trigger, an old CrossFit friend from his time in Florida sent him a message asking if he was OK. John hadn't heard from him since he left Florida, so he put the gun down and answered the message. His friend had no clue what was happening in that moment as they began to talk about what had transpired with Davina.

The ensuing hour-long conversation on the phone took John from the brink of suicide. He unloaded the gun and placed it back in the safe. That same night he began to search for answers on the internet, looking through various sites and articles. They put forward conflicting things about why women leave men and what men can do to get their women back. Surfing into the night, he came across a "Red Pill" Reddit forum, its name borrowed from *The Matrix*. As he opened the page, he saw a list of articles on the right (he was "reading the sidebar"). The forum was very active, with many posts from men much like John who were in the same situation. John's journey into the Red Pill was beginning.

John had quit drinking, and after two months of barely eating, he had dropped twenty-five pounds. His face was thinner, and he was trying to regrow his hair.

John needed to change his personal appearance, which had been bothering him for so long. He was focusing on his self-improvement, and although he was not ready for dating, he began seeing multiple women strictly for sex. He would no longer emotionally invest in women who could go "nuclear" on his family in an instant. John resented and hated how he had given so much power to Davina, allowing her to nearly destroy his life.

John had to move out of the house he had shared with Davina and found and bought a new home for him and the boys. The goal was to start a new life. John knew the breakup had deeply affected the boys; they cried constantly in the knowledge Davina had never loved them. John comforted them every night, explaining to them that it was not their fault and that he loved them dearly. In time the boys came to resent Davina much like John did. Even more painful was the fact that John worked in the same building as her and had to see her constantly with a new, unknown man.

Her appearance had drastically changed. She had grown her hair out, gained weight, and started to wear more feminine clothing—a stark contrast to the heavily tattooed, septum-pierced, shorthaired person he had known, the Davina who had often been perceived as a lesbian. The light-switch effect had not only ended their relationship but by all appearances had compelled her to try on a new identity.

When John briefly spoke with her, she was casual and nonchalant about her new life and completely disregarded John. She had an air of entitlement. When asked why she had left, one more time she responded, "Because you were not worth my investment." Whatever her intent with this statement, whether it was truthful or just an attempt to hurt him, this was exactly what John needed to hear to move on.

As time went on, they would casually pass each other in the halls, not as former lovers who had shared a life but as complete strangers. Of course, John could see the discomfort in Davina as they walked by each other, but he no longer had any fucks to give. He still loved her, but his life path was his own now, and he knew he needed to invest in himself and make himself better. John regretted ever having put a gun to his head for a woman. His heart was stone cold; the last remaining humanity he would only give to his sons.

He searched and read Red Pill content after Red Pill content on Reddit. Ingesting the sidebar, John was beginning to get the answers as to why everything happened the way it did. The problem was, John didn't like the answers. He had grown up with a certain way of thinking about women, which had been reinforced by Hollywood—the "chivalry" code of how to treat women. Although the Red Pill truths were hard for John to accept and understand as reality, he realized those uncomfortable truths affected his feelings more than his logic. Logically, everything made sense, even if it did go against the grain of what he thought he knew.

The Red Pill is the hardest pill any man can swallow. Not only does it change the way men think about how things wish or want them to be, but it also initiates a process of unplugging that shows the reality of what reality is. In *The Matrix*, Keanu Reeves is given the choice of two pills—the red pill, which will allow him to see how life really is, and the blue pill, which will allow him to remain blissfully unaware and return to his former life.

Author caveat: The information discussed in the following chapters is information derived from the book and blog The Rational Male *and from information discussed by Rollo Tomassi, Richard Cooper, Joker from the Better Bachelor, Coach Greg Adams, and Terrance Popp. This Red Pill information is what John learned during the unplugging process.*

Proceed with Caution

Once you take the Red Pill, you will forever be changed. Even if you attempt to spit the Red Pill out, you will never see life in the same "Blue Pill" way again. The process of unplugging from the Blue Pill is dangerous. Too many men want to cling to their false reality. Unplugging for John was not overly hard, mostly a confirmation of what he had already suspected from his experiences growing up, serving in the military, being in the police force, and experiencing his failed marriage with Amber.

His failed relationship with Davina was the final nail. John understood the idea that the best (and probably only) way to unplug was through pain. As has been repeatedly discussed on the forum, you cannot give Blue Pill men the Red Pill unless they are ready to accept it. Breaking men free from the narrative is dirty and dangerous.

John read the book *The Rational Male*, by the remarkable author Rollo Tomassi. After he had read his book and ingested the information, John's past experiences made sense. He figuratively took the Red Pill, knowing it was a death sentence for the Blue Pill version of his self. The Blue Pill version of John had died. John realized that everything he knew and thought he knew was born from a gynocentric social conditioning that had been built upon decades of lies perpetuated by Hollywood, social media, and society.

When discussing Red Pill, Blue Pill, Alpha, and Beta—these are placeholder terms. Each placeholder term is independent of the others. For example, an Alpha man can be Blue Pill, through a process known as "killing the Beta," which can be a matter of life or death for a man. The mind-set of a Blue Pill man can kill him under certain circumstances because his mind is ingrained in the old social contract way of thinking. Most men today cannot accept there is a new social contract.[1]

To understand Red Pill, John had to understand how Blue Pill idealism had conditioned him to follow a false narrative about intergender and social dynamics. One of the hardest things for John was to cut away from his old life and idealism, something he had been conditioned into while growing up. Hollywood fantasies are not real. John had to cut himself away from Blue Pill thoughts and idealism in order to grow. He needed to understand the reality of intergender and social dynamics and how they played out on a large social scale.

After taking the Red Pill, John understood where he had failed in every previous relationship. All it had taken was Rollo's book, an eloquent forum, and hundreds of hours of research—not to mention the collaborative effort of every Red Pill man on Reddit and YouTube. But John saw clearly that Rollo had been the first man to use words to connect the dots in order to form the reality of intersexual and social dynamics. John could easily relate to the Red Pill information. It was as if his eyes were open for the very first time. Everything John had seen, done, and observed from his military, police, and government background now had meaning and understanding.

The danger of Red Pill is the fact that once you see it and ingest it, you can never go back. You will see that everything in our lives is born from a Blue Pill social construction. It's a mentality where fantasies overcome reality. That's probably why there are many variations in how men swallow the pill. The Purple Pill is a mix of Red Pill and Blue Pill awareness. The Black Pill is a constant state of darkness and a reality that is cold, cruel, and harsh. The Red, Blue, Purple, and Black Pills each have their merits and means of suiting men's lives. For John, the Red Pill was the source of answers to pressing questions.

Rollo highlights the five stages of unplugging from a Blue Pill mind-set on his Rational Male blog forum. Listed succinctly, they are denial, anger, bargaining, depression, and acceptance. A sixth stage was added later on the forum. Jaded. But John's interpretation of the material included all six stages within the original five.[2] The transition from Blue Pill to Red Pill represented for John the death of his old self and ways of thinking; its stages were akin to the stages of grieving. This gave way to the rebirth of a new identity and way of thinking. Hence, when John internalized the Red Pill, he had a phoenix tattooed as a half sleeve on his left arm to signify his new self rising from the ashes.

John felt each of these emotions during his unplugging process, although not in the order illustrated on the forum. This process took months.

The first stage of unplugging John felt was denial. Initially John denied that what he was reading was an altruistic fact. This couldn't be real, because it conflicted with and went against the grain of the gynocentric idealism he had been brainwashed into believing since childhood.

He could not fathom how something so opposed to what he had thought he knew could be so contextually right and clearly illustrated through his life. The truth had been there all along; he just hadn't connected the dots, or internally he didn't want to connect the dots. Having experienced many of the same problems as other men, John refused to overlook what he had been through in the past. He could no longer deny himself the blatant truth anymore.

The second stage of unplugging—and the briefest for John—was bargaining. *Maybe if I accept some Red Pill awareness and apply it to the knowledge I already know, maybe that is where the truth really lies. Surely all women can't be this bad,* he thought. Even though John had experienced firsthand the nature of women based on his relationships with his mother, Julie, Susan, Amber, and Davina, he held onto the belief that not all women are like that (NAWALT).

Sure, he had chosen the wrong women in his life, but he had to hold out hope that he could still find a decent woman for a relationship. Maybe if he were a better person. Wealthier, better looking, taller, and not a single father, he would have been able to keep Davina in his life.

After a brief interlude, those thoughts quickly turned into his third stage of unplugging, depression. Ever since shaving his head bald, John had experienced low self-esteem. He felt unattractive and hated how bald guys were mocked and ridiculed. He was depressed and hurt that he had lost his soul mate out of the blue with no apparent reason. He reasoned that if he had had Red Pill awareness before Davina broke up with him, he could have saved the relationship. Everything he had learned growing up was a lie. He was supposed to be a good, nice man and be rewarded for being a gentleman. That's how he grew up thinking intersexual dynamics worked.

In reality being a "nice guy" is a vagina repellent, creating a sub-Saharan desert between a woman's legs. It was depressing for him to think that women don't want the nice guy who is there for them—supporting them emotionally, ensuring their financial security, always caring for and protecting them (chivalry). Instead John realized they want the asshole Alpha Chad or Tyrone who makes them tingle, even as they complain they can't find any good men.

The dichotomy of it all was so confusing to John. *So why bother being a nice guy when I would have more options as an asshole?* he asked.

This thought process transitioned John from the bargaining phase to the anger phase. John wasn't necessarily angry at what had happened to him in the past. He was angrier at himself for not having been able to connect the dots or understand innately that what he thought he knew was completely wrong. He had never heard the term intersexual dynamics until gaining Red Pill awareness. With a new Red Pill lens, he could understand the process of cultural indoctrination.

The anger consumed him, and he hated women for being the exact opposite of what he thought they were. He thought women were the ones who valued love and commitment, only to realize the fact that men love idealistically, while women love opportunistically. A man's idea of love and having a family was idealistic, based on the notion that whatever he gave to a woman she would ultimately give back to him.

John realized that in fact women "pretend" to love the man for who he is, but in reality women love the opportunities men can provide them. Men are idealists, while women are realists. A man would list out the things he has done for his woman, while a woman thinks, what has he done for me now? There is a clear difference between how men and women think and operate within the sexual marketplace and intersexual relationships.

Within the anger phase, John became very jaded toward women. He would use dating as an active tool to practice the game, learn real-world intersexual dynamics, and never maintain a serious relationship. He would talk with several women at once, all on a rotation, with no real interest in developing a long-term relationship (this is known as "spinning plates"). To John, women were no longer worth any investment and were strictly a liability. During this time, John had gone MGTOW (Men Going Their Own Way) and focused on his own self-improvement.

John continued to singlehandedly raise his sons while simultaneously improving his physical appearance. Hours upon hours in the gym and a hair transplant. Participating in races, improving his financial status, and focusing on improving his personal and professional knowledge. This was his time to overhaul everything. The Red Pill not only changed his thought process but also changed him forever as a man. A man whom Davina could never have again. John knew he could no longer accept her back into his life. He was no longer the man she once knew, and any thought of rekindling a relationship dissipated from his mind.

The hardest part of ingesting the Red Pill for John was the fact that he could not seem to get out of the anger phase. It was almost like a dark, barren wasteland; there seemed to be no real reason to ever trust a woman again, let alone be in a long-term relationship with one. There was no point to any of it, because love comes and goes. Thoughts of "She's not yours; it's just your turn" were ingrained in his mind.

This was especially true when a woman professed her love to John. He knew when a woman said she loved him that it meant she loved him "right now." To John, a woman's love was worth a grain of salt. John had been told by many women that they loved him. He silently added the words "right now" after each one. He knew these women loved him for what he could provide for them, but they did not love him for who he was as a man. A woman's love can be turned on and turned off as quickly as the flip of a light. Besides, love fades, as illustrated in his failed relationships with Susan, Amber, and Davina.

Having crossed the barren wasteland of self-loathing anger and ingrained hatred for women, John reached the final phase of unplugging, acceptance. John had come to accept women's nature and instead of hating them thought of this nature as part of the game. Knowing he could either love women or understand them, he consciously chose to understand them. He knew he would never idealistically love another woman again, in the way he had loved Susan, Amber, and Davina. It was counterintuitive within his new Red Pill understanding of intersexual dynamics. John's social conditioning out of Blue Pill idealism was complete.

CHAPTER 10

Through his Red Pill journey, John's awareness of intersexual dynamics based on a gynocentric society continued to grow. For John to grow emotionally and intellectually, he had to dissect his personal experiences and critically self-reflect on where he had gone wrong. This allowed him to fully understand the how and why of the failure of all his previous relationships. One of the very first misconceptions John had to accept was the soul mate myth. There is no "one." There are good women and bad women, but there is no "one woman" who is some predestined soul mate. Men who develop this idealistic attachment to their "one" suffer from what is known as ONEitis.[3]

Although John never had ONEitis for Susan or Amber, he had been deeply infected with the thought that Davina was his "one," his soul mate. His thoughts of how they were meant to be together forever only shattered when she easily and coldly left. ONEitis is an idealized fantasy perpetuated by Disney, Hollywood, and music.

The thought that fate and the universe perfectly align with the intention of causing two people to meet—this is Blue Pill romanticism. The bases of the "one" as that perfect individual you were meant to be with. As if some preordained alignment of twin souls who would meet and could be together forever was even possible. Robin Williams in *What Dreams May Come* is a perfect example. I mean, the cosmos would never be wrong about two souls predestined to be together, would it?

Dispelling relationship magic, the Red Pill reality centers on the fact that ONEitis is an unhealthy emotional and psychological dependence transferred from one person onto another (i.e., a perceived soul mate). This unhealthy way of thinking is reinforced and mass marketed in the current Western society; it is considered a healthy aspect of a marriage and other long-term relationships, which could not be further from the truth. It is an unhealthy codependence that might have devastating and deadly consequences should that relationship end and the "soul mate" leave their partner.

John never thought he could live without Davina until he was forced to. His idealized relationship was down the tubes, and when the dust settled, he was empty. A void he should have filled with his own love was filled and removed by the one he considered his soul mate. That void zeroed John out, leading him to think his only other option was to commit suicide. John's Blue Pill mind-set was so ingrained with the soul mate myth, he had thought of killing himself over losing his soul mate rather than realizing it was the end of a relationship and that he was free to seek new opportunities elsewhere.

As Rollo points out, "There is no greater agency for a woman than to know beyond doubt that she is the only source of a man's need for sex and intimacy...For a man who believes that the emotionally and psychologically damaging relationship he has ego-invested himself is with the only person in his lifetime he's ever going to be compatible with, there is nothing more paralyzing in his maturation."[4] ONEitis doesn't only affect men; it affects women as well.

Ever hear the Katy Perry song "The One That Got Away"? In the song a married old woman reflects on her past, how her "one" got away, as her "soul mate" had been killed years earlier in a car accident. Even decades after his death, she cannot not move on or get over him, even though she is married to another man. This soul mate mentality literally plagues her for the rest of her life. This arguably has affected her current marriage because her husband cannot compete with the "one who got away."

The idea of a soul mate is a myth perpetuated by social conditioning. When John accepted that there was no "one," it allowed him to have a healthier understanding of choosing future partners. He understood that there was no soul mate out in the universe waiting to find him. Think about a time in your life where you had someone you perceived as the "one" or your soul mate. How did that affect your perception of that person?

Accepting this reality, John also realized one of the great cardinal rules of relationships, whether social, professional, or romantic—the fact is that the person who holds the most power in the relationship is the one who needs the other person the least. The power to walk away. This is a "dot" that many people can see but may not fully understand. In the case of John's personal experience, Davina held the power in their relationship. He knew she hadn't needed John like he needed and wanted her. The person who can walk away without a second thought holds the power in any relationship.

Although it may thus be misconstrued that power equals dominance, this is not the case. Take, for example, a buyer at a car dealership. The person needing a car relinquishes power to the dealership. However, a person wanting a car maintains his power. He has the power to walk away if the deal is not good enough for his financial investment. The power and ability to walk away from someone or something who does not serve your investment is vital to maintaining self-agency and mental point of origin.

John was astounded by how much power he had given Davina in their relationship. He also realized through Red Pill awareness how he had never made himself his own mental point of origin. He had placed her on a pedestal, thinking of himself as secondary; thinking what he did was the right thing to do instead of thinking of himself first. The concept of mental point of origin is removed from boys as they grow into adulthood. Don't be selfish, because that may hurt other people's feelings. John was taught to think of family first and himself last.

In the current gynocentric social order, men are always required to put their families before themselves.

Let's look through a historical lens—during the sinking of the Titanic, women and children were given priority on the lifeboats. What is more intrinsically valuable in a survival situation? Sperm is considered cheap, so men are socially accepted as expendable. Eggs are considered valuable, so they must be protected, while children are the future. But a child on its own typically cannot survive. So the next logical choice in our gynocentric way of thinking is giving priority to women, who have expensive eggs to nurture and can care for the children. Today in our current social construct, men are expendable, and it's deemed chivalrous to be so.

Accepting this fact is a hard truth to swallow. Men are expected to be chivalrous and held to pre–sexual revolution standards. Feminism allowed women to exploit this newfound power to elevate themselves above men. To be considered a "real man" (or for a man to be respected by current social standards), a man must be able to rationally solve problems. Men must provide resources to women and children, be chivalrous and willing to sacrifice their lives for what society deems a worthy cause. In the current social structure, men are held 100 percent accountable and responsible with 0 percent authority.

The chivalry code once used on the battlefields long ago was a code of honor and integrity between opponents. That concept has been changed to suit the needs of the feminine imperative. In today's mainstream culture, it is the primary way for a gynocentric society to measure a man's traditional masculinity. The social conventions of today use masculinity to serve the feminine purpose. When masculinity is not perfectly aligned with serving the needs of the feminine imperative, it is considered "toxic" masculinity or misogyny. We are in an age where masculinity is not defined by men but defined by an over feminized, gynocentric society.

John and millions of other men were taught to provide unearned and default respect for women. To never hit girls because they are, by contemporary definitions, the "fairer" sex. They are "weaker" than men, and men are supposed to provide for and protect them. The simple fact is that women do not automatically deserve respect just because they are women. This elevates them above men and overly inflates their egos, feeding their entitled nature.

When elevated on a pedestal, they have no place to look but down, and a woman can never respect a man she looks down on. She only respects a man she can look up to. If you treat her like a rock star, she will treat you as a fan. A woman only has to exist to have respect, while a man must earn respect. Any man who deviates from this social construct is shamed and labeled a misogynist, chauvinist, or one of a range of other insulting labels. Shame is the best tactic to realign men to "do the right thing," say the right thing, and conform to social narratives.

By putting Davina on a pedestal, John had doomed their relationship. It wasn't that he should have known better; he was doing what had been ingrained into this Blue Pill psyche. His early mind-set was reinforced by gynocentric imperatives, blatantly displayed, advertised, and pushed as a social agenda within TV, movies, music, literature, and marketing. Men who go against the grain and do not give undeserved respect to women are shamed and chastised.

John was able to see how many Blue Pill mistakes he had made as he reflected on his failed relationship with Davina through a Red Pill lens. There are two types of reality—the idealistic one into which we are socially programmed, known as Blue Pill conditioning, and the Red Pill, which accepts reality for what it really is, what is biologically imprinted subconsciously in our DNA. The current gynocentric social construct goes against our biological hardwiring, which has been refined over thousands of years.

While at work, John would walk the halls with colleagues or grab lunch from the cafeteria and, not even a couple weeks postbreakup, see Davina with a new man alongside her. It became directly apparent to John why she had left him and why she had already moved on. It wasn't because she had needed to "find herself," as she had claimed. She had left John when she had become sure the other man was a solid option to swing to, an act known as "monkey branching."

When a heterosexual woman says she needs to "find herself," she either already has or is looking for other, better options (men)—or she is cheating. There is no in-between. "Finding oneself" is a term used by women to justify that they are exploring all other options besides you. There is a hypergamous doubt in her mind that you are not her best option. So, when she needs to "find herself," she's already found or is on the lookout for that better option. Although it's hard for men to understand why a woman could be hot one minute and cold the next, there are many variables that exist in the back of her mind that most men are not aware of or don't understand.

Understanding a female's nature is not all that difficult. Hollywood and Disney have Blue Pill–conditioned generations of men into believing women are mysterious. Once you see through the "mystery" and understand female nature for what it is, then you can truly understand a woman. Again, you can love a woman, or you can understand them, but you can't do both. This may sound nihilistic, but understanding a woman's nature allows men to remove idealistic "love" and take a more pragmatic approach to developing and maintaining relationships with women.

One tenet of female nature John learned within the Red Pill community was a woman's hypergamous filter. Biologically hardwired in her brain, a woman's hypergamous filter is the voice or "feeling" she has when seeking a mate for short-term or long-term relationships and intimacy. The question being, Is he really the best I can do? Although a simple question on its surface, it becomes much more complex when you dissect the variables that presage it. Throughout her life a woman will fluctuate in her criteria and priorities based on whatever condition she may find herself in.

These conditions change over time as her sexual viability with men decreases, a factor known as sexual market value (SMV). An attractive woman who is twenty years old will have more sexual selection of partners than the forty-year-old version of herself. While in her youth and peak fertility phase, she is the selector from a large pool of partners whom she has deemed worthy of her intimacy. As she gets older and her fertility wanes, the pool of prospective partners decreases. A woman's optimal SMV window exists when she is between eighteen and twenty-eight years old (her party years), peaking when she's between twenty-four and twenty-five.

A woman between twenty-eight and thirty is in what is known as the epiphany phase. This is when it's time for her to settle down and lock in a long-term provider with whom to start a family, if she hasn't already had kids with another man. This is also known as the "biological clock" that is ever ticking in the back of a woman's mind. The problem is, when she reaches the epiphany phase, her ability to find the men she could have had during her peak years has waned. Her conditions and priorities have changed, and her strategy to lock down a provider must evolve as well. Because her pool of potential mates has decreased, her criteria for a long-term partner must evolve to solve for her long-term sexual mating strategy.

She still wants that hot Alpha man who gives her the tingles, but her ability to attract those men into a long-term relationship is compromised, since they have younger options and she's aged out of the sexual marketplace. So, to fulfill her long-term mating strategy, she seeks out the security of the Beta male, who may be her best option now but would not have been during her peak fertility years. She has given her best years and sex to hot Alpha men, while Beta men get what's left over.

Women make rules for Betas and break rules for Alphas, full stop. What many Blue Pill–conditioned men don't realize is that although women hold the keys to sexual intimacy, men hold the keys to relationships. Women use their sexual agency to entice the man into providing a long-term relationship. "This is why there is nothing more threatening yet simultaneously attractive to a woman than a man who is aware of his own value to women. Women don't want a man to cheat, but they want a man who could cheat."[5] Furthermore "nothing is more satisfying for a woman to have a man other women desire and for her to think her feminine intuition has figured her man out."[6]

Within a woman's hypergamous filter is the desire she has for her partner. Another thing many men do not realize is you can never, ever negotiate desire. I will say that again—*you can never, ever negotiate desire.* A woman who has natural, carnal desire for her partner has satisfied one part of her hypergamous filter. As Kyle Reese explained to Sarah Connor in the original *Terminator,* "Listen and understand. That terminator is out there. It can't be bargained with. It can't be reasoned with. It doesn't feel pity, or remorse, or fear. And it absolutely will not stop, ever, until you are dead."[7] The same can be said for a woman's hypergamy and carnal desire. Hypergamy and desire cannot be bargained with. They can't be reasoned with. Hypergamy and desire do not feel pity or remorse for any partner who does not measure up to a woman's biological instincts.

This brings us into Briffault's Law, which maintains that "the female, not the male, determines all the conditions of the animal family. Where the female can derive no benefit from association with the male, no such association takes place."[8] If the carnal desire that fulfills a woman's hypergamous filter is not present, or there is no benefit she can receive from a man, this goes against her hypergamous mind. She will not waste time on a man who cannot satisfy her biological imperative. The biological clock is always ticking. Ticktock. Ticktock.

The most important thing a man must understand about hypergamy is that hypergamy does *not* care. If you are not answering her hypergamous doubt, no matter the circumstances and no matter how much relational equity you think you have with her, she will find a more fulfilling option. There are no ifs, ands, or buts about this. She is always looking for the best option. It does not matter if you have been in a short-term relationship for months or a long-term relationship for years. Hypergamy does *not* care. She will not have any feelings of guilt as long as her hypergamous imperative is satisfied by her best option.

Hypergamy does not care if you are the best father in the world. It does not care if you have changed your life path or career to be with her. It does not care how supportive you are as a husband or how much you have based your decisions on accommodating her. Hypergamy does not care how long you have been married, or how emotionally invested you are in a relationship. Hypergamy does not care what religious views you and she share, the money you invested in her by paying off her bills, or whether the children you helped raise are yours or not.

Hypergamy does not care how much you are loved by friends and family. It does not care how many chores you do around the house and certainly does not care how "good" of a man you thought you were with her. Hypergamy does not care about the breakfasts in bed, the vacations, the romantic times you shared. Hypergamy does not care about your qualities as a person or how she left the relationship for no apparent reason (which you never saw coming). Hypergamy does not care if she cheats with your best friend or coworker. Hypergamy does not care.[9]

The reason hypergamy does not care is because in her mind, you were not her best option. She left because she will not want to waste time before moving on to a better or more appealing option. Ticktock. Ticktock. A woman will monkey branch to another man whom she feels answers her hypergamous doubt. If her grip on the other option proves not as strong as she thought, she will swing back to you and try to "make things work." It's the security net for her in case all else fails. However, don't think for one second she has stopped looking for a more suitable and attractive option to satisfy her hypergamous question.

Hypergamy does not care how much a man has sacrificed and invested in a woman. For men, there is this perceived unwritten rule of honor known as relationship equity.[10] This is where a man will devote time and resources into a relationship expecting a return on the investment. Every good thing he does is like a coin being put into a bank account, which can be drawn from during times of trouble or when "I'm not happy" comes out of her mouth. The investment does not have a return. Your bank account balance is still zero, and it's not about what you have done for her. The question on her mind is "What can he do or what has he done for me now?"

Another hard truth to swallow is hypergamy does not care if you cheat. As long as you are her very best option—the best she has ever had (or hoped to get)—and answer her hypergamous doubt. This is the only time hypergamy forgives. So as a man, use her hypergamy against her by being the very best man (option) she could ever hope to have. Remember, as a man you have the burden of performance, and if you are not performing, hypergamy will *not* care. If you are her very best option and you leave her, she will forever pine over the "one that got away." This is known as the "Alpha widow" phenomenon.

John had experienced hypergamy three separate times with Susan, Amber, and Davina. He just didn't know the definition then or even that there was such a thing. When he went on a six-month deployment only to come back to a "cold" Susan claiming she was sick, he was in fact dealing with the fact that she was seeing another man. She saw the new prospect as a better option than John, only to come back to John when the other man proved to be a downgrade.

This is also where John should have learned that there is no such thing as a long-distance relationship (LDR). No matter how much you try to convince yourself that your relationship is an exception, one party or the other is still seeking better options, maximizing or minimizing sexual strategies.

Amber, for instance, saw John as the better option as compared to her previous boyfriend. Davina, as we have seen, saw another coworker as a better option than John. This other man answered her hypergamous doubts about John, and she went nuclear on an entire family just to pursue this new option, without a moment's hesitation. Thus Susan and Davina had no problem leaving John to pursue what they perceived as better options based on their hypergamous filters.

As a man navigating the sexual marketplace, it is vital to understand the "game" and apply it, even if you are married or in a long-term relationship. Women want a man who just "gets it."[11] Women don't want a man who needs to be told how to play the game and don't want to be told in turn. Women want to play the game naturally. Women want a man who just gets it, and although you will see many women on dating profiles who seem to value honesty in a man, these same women don't want *full disclosure*.

In his book *The Rational Male* and on his *Rational Male* blog, Rollo distinctly outlines nine "iron rules" meant to help men navigate the sexual marketplace.

IRON RULE OF TOMASSI #1

Frame is everything. Always be aware of the subconscious balance of whose frame in which you are operating.

Always control the Frame, but resist giving the impression that you are.

IRON RULE OF TOMASSI # 2
NEVER, under pain of death, honestly or dishonestly reveal the number of women you've slept with or explain any detail of your sexual experiences with them to a current lover.

IRON RULE OF TOMASSI #3
Any woman who makes you wait for sex, or by her actions implies she is making you wait for sex; the sex is NEVER worth the wait.

IRON RULE OF TOMASSI #4
NEVER under any circumstance live with a woman you aren't married to or are not planning to marry in within 6 months.

IRON RULE OF TOMASSI #5
NEVER allow a woman to be in control of the birth.

IRON RULE OF TOMASSI #6
Women are utterly incapable of loving a man in the way that a man expects to be loved.

IRON RULE OF TOMASSI #7
It is always time and effort better spent developing new, fresh, prospective women than it will ever be in attempting to reconstruct a failed relationship. Never root

through the trash once the garbage has been dragged to the curb. You get messy, your neighbors see you do it, and what you thought was worth digging for is never as valuable as you thought it was.

IRON RULE OF TOMASSI #8
Always let a woman figure out why she won't fuck you, never do it for her.

IRON RULE OF TOMASSI #9
Never Self-Deprecate under any circumstance. This is a Kiss of Death that you self-initiate and is the antithesis of the Prize Mentality. Once you've accepted yourself and presented yourself as a "complete douche" there's no going back to confidence with a woman.[12]

John had broken every single one of Rollo's rules within his relationships. It's not that he meant to, he just did not have the knowledge available to him at that time to learn and realize he was making cardinal mistakes within every relationship. Thus none of his relationships lasted. It was the unwritten rules he had no knowledge of; he had only the knowledge of what he thought he was supposed to be, having grown up in a feminized, gynocentric, Blue Pill–conditioned state.

John began to use his eyes for the very first time. Through foresight he could see everything he had done right and everything he had done wrong in all three relationships. It was like a light bulb going off in his head. He was ashamed and embarrassed that he had not seen the signs or connected the dots earlier. Everything made perfect sense, and he could see how *The Rational Male* and the Red Pill community were absolutely right about female nature. It was as if they had a written the content with a microscope on his life.

John understood the cold, hard truths of reality and how truths don't give a shit about your opinion or *your* truth. Having come to understand Red Pill concepts and having swallowed the Red Pill, John decided to apply the Red Pill knowledge he was learning to his life and dating. John had had a lot of success with women in the past, having slept with well over one hundred women before he was in a relationship with Davina. Yet in the age of online dating apps including Tinder, Bumble, and Plenty of Fish, to name a few, John had entered an entirely new reality; he had last been single in 2012.

There was no way John was going to immediately jump into another long-term relationship. He had been burned too many times, and now he could see the blatant truths before his eyes. He was done with women and only used them for one purpose and one purpose only. He needed time to rebuild himself and his life. Adding a long-term partner into the mix was not a viable option, as women were now seen more as a liability. The cost-benefit ratio of having a steady girlfriend was not worth his investment. John certainly didn't lack for options with women, and he wasn't interested in being monogamous, especially since sex was so easy to obtain.

John understood when you take away the sexual agency of a woman in a relationship, there were no other aspects in which women would complement his life. He was a very good cook, kept a neat and clean home, held a professional career, and had an extensive educational background. He was free to do anything he wanted, whenever he wanted, without having to deal with another person or her drama. The only benefit of having a woman for John was sex. The prospect of settling down was not really an option for him. The juice was simply not worth the squeeze in his opinion.

This is where John learned about the male movement MGOTW. This movement stresses self-ownership and modern-day men protecting and preserving their own sovereignty above anything else by making themselves their own mental point of origin. It is the rejection of preconceptions of social and cultural definitions and expectations of what it is to be a man. The refusal to bow to, serve, or kneel to women who view and use men as a disposable utility. It's life well served according to a man's own boundaries and in service of his own best interests. It is the complete rejection of the new and old social contracts; marriage, having families, and long-term relationships are now only seen as liabilities and not additions to men's lives. These men live for their own purpose and, unlike married men, truly allow themselves to be alone, independent, and self-reliant. Today a real test for a man is not in families or marriages but in his ability to live and be completely comfortable with himself.

Droves of men are being drawn into the MGTOW movement, most after having been through the family court system and divorce machine. Often these men were married for years only to have their wives tell them they were unhappy and divorce them. And with the pull of a pin on the marriage grenade, the court system rewards these women with alimony, child support, and, typically, full custody of the children, while the man must forfeit half of anything he earns. There is such a big incentive for women to divorce their husbands and thus win cash prizes; it is thus no surprise that, according to the National Center for Health Statistics, about 50 percent of marriages in the United States end in divorce. About 80 percent of these divorces are initiated by women.

It's no wonder men are tired of being run through the court system, losing everything they have built up and worked for their entire lives (this includes the loss of access to parenting their children). It's like jumping out of an airplane with a fifty-fifty chance the parachute will open. Men no longer see the value in the risk of being married in our current society. In the current social climate, the court system, divorce and custody laws, and social constructs make marriage a very dangerous prospect for those still willing to embark upon it.

There is no real benefit of marriage for men today. The old social contract of marriage died with the onset of feminism and sexual freedom. Before the sexual revolution, men and women were required by the old social contract to be married before they engaged in any sexual activity. With the onset of the sexual revolution, feminism, and birth control, the entire social contract changed forever. Men and women were now free to sexually express themselves with whomever they chose outside the commitment of marriage. For the first time in human history, women were directly in charge of the reproductive process.

Before the introduction of birth control, women who had children outside of marriage were socially cast out. With the introduction of birth control, women were free to experience sexual freedom without the repercussions of unwanted pregnancy. This, combined with the growing feminist movement, set the stage for the creation of the new social contract. The new social contract we are experiencing today illustrates an imbalance in relationships between men and women, in which it is blatantly clear that neither side is happy. This is because the roles of men and women have changed, and this has destroyed a millennium of biological hardwiring.

Women have already adapted to this new social contract. Unfortunately, men have not caught up to speed and realized women operate under the new social contract. Most men still operate according to the long-destroyed, old social contract. This is apparent within the sexual marketplace of modern dating. Advancements in technology, dating apps, and social media have paved a new way of social interaction between men and women. Never before has there been such an ease of access to information and people. One of many consequences of this is the destruction of intersexual relationships between men and women.

For the first time in history, men and women are now competing against each other—not only in the sexual marketplace but in the workplace and every other space men and women share. The natural biological order has been removed. Men and women are no longer complements (old social contract) to each other but competitors (new social contract). In the premodern age of our grandparents, complementary relationships between husband and wife were essential to the survival of the family unit. Men were the protectors who provided security and stability for their family. It was essential for a family's survival that the man care for and provide for his family, even if this cost him his life (old social contract).

In a postmodern age where technology reigns supreme, men are considered no longer needed. Women no longer need protection and provisioning from a man for their survival. A woman is able to work and provide her own financial security with a social construct protecting her physical security. She is able to live a free and independent lifestyle, with full control over her reproductive rights (childbirth or abortion). Heard the phrase "her body, her choice"? She no longer needs a man for reproduction, as she can go to any sperm bank, choose the best specimen for her, and be artificially inseminated.

Men are now seen as disposable utilities, so it is no wonder intersexual relationships have changed for the worse. Men must understand that women do not want equality. Women want all of the privileges of being a woman and all of the privileges of being a man (their version of equality), without the responsibilities of either. Feminists do not feel they need to do anything for the expressed pleasure of a man, while simultaneously living out their best years partying and sleeping with multiple partners because hey, men can do that; why can't they?

When discussing modern dating and relationships, women still fully expect men to abide by the old social contract. The man should be a chivalrous gentleman, generous with his time and resources without expecting anything in return. The new social contract is, again, women wanting all of the privileges of being a woman without having the responsibilities of one. Equality between men and women has already been achieved when discussing equal opportunity in a social, educational, and workplace context.

However, equality does not exist in the sexual marketplace or in the scope of intersexual dynamics. In every relationship there is a leader who takes charge and a follower who submits to the leader. This is a complementary relationship; no relationship can function if there is a power struggle between the two parties vying for leadership. A complementary relationship is made of trust and respect. Both parties are responsible for their roles within the relationship. Unfortunately, that was the old social contract. Although still desperately clung to by men, it is no longer socially applicable within the current gynocentric society.

CHAPTER 11

B reaking free from Blue Pill idealism, John was freed from the social constraints that had once bound his mind into putting women above his own self-interests. He continued to actively date, navigate the SMP, and sleep around with many women (over eighty-five women in a year following the breakup with Davina); John continued to focus on his sons and his career while still having to deal with his ex-wife Amber.

Having fully ingested the Red Pill, John wanted his sons to grow into strong, intelligent young men who knew their value. To always seek self-improvement and not accept mediocrity. Comfort causes complacency. John was firm but fair in how he raised his sons. He worked incredibly hard to maintain a household on his own, even while receiving no support from Amber. John would help them with their homework, teach them self-defense, run long distances as they biked with him and carried water. They were a very active team, doing everything together as a family.

Single parenting was tough for John because he had to juggle his career alongside his sons, pays the bills, and ensure the boys were raised right according to his beliefs. Better than how he had been raised based on the Blue Pill mentality. John was going to slowly infuse Red Pill awareness into each of his sons so they would not make the same mistakes he had made. He wanted to show them their own intrinsic value. John was going to ensure his sons had a realistic awareness of life and how to operate within the current social construct. He would ensure that they had the tools and knowledge necessary for future success.

As a single father dating in the sexual marketplace, John knew there were going to be challenges. Armed with Red Pill knowledge, John accepted the "game" for what it was, not how he wanted it to be. Dating had certainly changed—or had dating always been this difficult? In either case, now he was able to observe and experience it with his new awareness. John knew his intrinsic value on the dating market and what he brought to the table. He was very good looking, very physically fit, and successful in his career with the government (which any man would be envious of). He was financially stable, owned his own home and vehicle, and had a solid educational background.

For John, having access to this information as he entered his peak SMV years was invaluable. He was able to see women for what they were—the good and the bad. He now understood that he had been participating in the "game" without knowing the rules, which was exactly why all three of his previous serious relationships had failed. He now fully understood the rules of the game, which immensely helped him navigate the sexual marketplace, spotting immediate red flags in women he otherwise would have entertained as prospects.

Knowledge is power, and not only had this knowledge given him invaluable insight but it had also made him a better man for understanding how intersexual dynamics work from a nonfemininized, nongynocentric mind-set. Although John knew he could never have the idealistic kind of love he thought he wanted from his previous relationships, he realized he could now be much happier and more emotionally intelligent in future romantic relationships. However, he would be much more cautious before ever thinking about the word "commitment" again now that he understood female nature.

John was thirty-six years old, and his peaking SMV was an enticing prospect for any woman claiming to want a relationship. He realized that he was a prize for women and that women were a complement to his life, not the sole focus of it. A complete contrast to the lessons of his upbringing, which had made him think that women were the prize.

Women only have a certain amount of eggs and a limited time of value in the sexual marketplace. Time was on his side, and he recognized that as he swiped right on profile after profile, there was always a common theme. Women who had entered or were entering the epiphany phase or were postwall (thirty years old and above) wrote on their dating profiles that they wanted something "real" and were not looking for hookups or games.

Women who claim they are not looking for hookups or to play games have already ridden the cock carousel hard during their early party years, their youth and beauty deteriorating with every passing year as they focused on their careers, party after party, riding cock after cock, their notch count ever increasing. Instead of having used their peak SMV to cash in on the high-value men who showed them attention, these women have been indoctrinated by feminism to believe they had plenty of time to land and secure a high-value man for a relationship.

Men of high value value youth, beauty, and femininity first and foremost. Men do not care how much education women have or about their careers (masculine traits). Many modern women assume a high level of education and a high-powered career gives them the ability to attract high-status men. This could not be further from the truth. The truth is these traits only limit a woman's dating options.

There are exceptions to every rule. However, women date equal to or up to their own perceived status and almost never date down. A woman CEO is not going to consider a man working in a fast food restaurant as a viable dating option. A woman respects a man who is above her in career and status. Remember the pedestal—women cannot respect a man they look down upon.

With so many women brainwashed into putting their careers ahead of their biological instincts, the short seven-year window between eighteen and twenty-five closes very quickly. This is even worse when a woman's SMV is realistically evaluated on her looks, weight, and femininity, not on her overinflated, perceived sense of self-worth.

This overinflated sense of self-worth is continually perpetuated by social media, TV shows, magazines, and Hollywood. It is also reinforced with current social conventions about "fat" shaming, "slut" shaming, and other phrases that attempt to normalize their deficiencies. Not only does it normalize their behavior and attitudes but it also silences any voices that go against this grain.

The sexual marketplace is much different for men. Women just are; men must become.[13] This is a slow-burn effect that leads a motivated man who becomes successful, stays in shape, is financially secure, and the like to reach his SMV peak in his midthirties. Women, on the other hand, have already peaked in their early twenties and slowly lose SMV until they hit the proverbial wall. Typically in their thirties these women realize they cannot attract men of the same status they could when in their early twenties and shame younger women when they are seen dating older men. Again, women want to have the same privileges as men in the sexual marketplace, but human biology says something different.

Women are under the assumption that because men are celebrated for sleeping with multiple women, a man who sleeps with many women is considered a "hero," whereas a woman who sleeps with many men would be considered a "slut." This is an accurate assumption based on our basic biologic levels. Men and women's minds are hardwired differently. High-value men do not want to invest in a long-term relationship with a woman who has ridden the cock carousel. Not only is it unattractive for the man to know his woman has been with many partners, it is mentally damaging for the woman as well.

Because men and women are hardwired differently, men can still form a pair bond attachment with a woman after sleeping with hundreds of women. The same cannot be said for women who have slept with hundreds of men. This is why virginity for men is of extreme importance. When a woman has had one or two male partners, she can pair bond with her man. The more partners she has had, the less she will be able to pair bond with that man. Instead of considering him her first and "best," a woman who has been with hundreds of men will always measure her current man according to the best traits of every man she's ever had.

With each new notch in her cock count, her hypergamy is left open to keep looking for a man who can be the embodiment of all the best men she's ever had, which she statistically will never find. It comes back to the same hypergamous question: Is he really the best I can do? When women complain about men's sexual promiscuity in the sexual marketplace, women do not understand that men have a much harder time sleeping around than women realize. For a woman to have sex with a man, if she's mildly attractive, all she has to do is say yes. Men are the ones who have to put in the work, time, and effort before a woman says yes.

It is much more difficult for men to have sex than women. This is why men who have the opportunity to sleep with a lot of women are seen as valuable men. When a man opens a woman's sexual intimacy, it's a case of winning the genetic lottery and the result of effort. As the saying goes, a lock that can be opened with many keys (dicks) is not a valuable lock. A key that can open many locks (vaginas) is a valuable key. This is why women in the sexual marketplace only reserve their sexual intimacy for top-tier, high-status men. It's the eighty-twenty rule: women will chase and pursue the top 20 percent of men over the bottom 80 percent.

Thus hypergamy cannot afford to be wrong. It's a biological imperative women mate with the best men they can attract. Women want a good man for security and the bad boy for sex because of the tingles. Rarely will a woman find both of those traits in one man. The Alpha fucks (bad boys) are the ones women pursue even knowing they are typically noncommittal, dangerous, or just exciting to be around. This solves her short-term mating strategy, while the Beta buck (provisioner) is a safe security net for her long-term sexual strategy. A woman will give starfish duty sex to the Beta provider. As Coach Greg Adams says, "Monkey double back flips" for the Alpha. Women absolutely love a competent, dominant, and primal man. That's where she gets the tingles.

"But not all women are like that (NAWALT)," exclaims literally every single woman. Many single, heterosexual, married women would love to have a sexual opportunity with a top-tier Alpha man (insert their freebie celebrity crush) should the opportunity arise. Is that celebrity crush a good long-term prospect? More than likely not, but a one-time encounter with that celebrity crush will live in her mind forever, whereas the dutiful sex she must give her husband to keep him satisfied won't.

In the dating market, women have a wide variety of options at their disposal. They are inundated with attention in online dating apps and via messages and likes in their social media accounts. Even intrinsically low-value women have options. This is because there has been such a drastic change in the sexual marketplace; thirsty men can be seen everywhere. They are the men who have no options, are not spinning any plates, and are still operating under the old social contract. Thirsty men validate women with, if nothing else, the amount of attention they give women with undeserved compliments; the attention further increases a woman's social proof and validates her ego.

Woman can spot a thirsty man a mile away, and there is nothing more unappealing or unattractive for her than to know this man doesn't have any options. Again, thirsty men validate her ego, but that's as far as they will ever get with her. She knows she can do better based on the amount of attention she receives. Thirsty men become one of a hundred. There is nothing special about them to make them stand out or warrant her attention and sexual intimacy. On the other hand, a man who is not thirsty, has a lot of options, and is his own mental point of origin is deemed a valuable man, an Alpha who will certainly warrant her attention, at least initially. A woman is naturally her own mental point of origin.

A woman will chase a man of value. Men of high value and social proof have no need to pursue women. A woman likes a challenge just as men love a challenge, if pursuing the woman in question is worth his time and investment. However, there being a very short supply of available, high-value men, the only men who really do the pursuing are not of high value. They are putting the pursuit of a woman ahead of their own goals. Again, women are a complement to a well-lived life, not the focus or center of it.

Women in your life will come and go. If you make them the center of life, what is left when the woman leaves? She is never yours; it's just your turn. This is why women are complementary. If she leaves you, you are free to pursue further options. Men of high value know their worth and continually pursue excellence. You cannot grow as a man in mediocrity, and typically the most growth a man can experience is through pain. Pain is inevitable; suffering is optional. Every person will experience pain in his life. How he chooses to cope and grow from that experience is on him.

John had experienced a lot of pain growing up. His life was filled with pain and violence from what he had seen and done in the Marines, in the police department, and while working for the government. Because of the Red Pill, John was able to understand and accept everything life had thrown at him. Navigating the sexual marketplace was no exception. Taking what he had learned, he came to recognize red flags as he saw them on the dating market. First and foremost, he realized the pecking order of a man's value as perceived by women.

Men love women; women love children; children love pets. That is the pecking order in any relationship. But NAWALT, right? In a disaster situation where life and death hang in the balance, the child will hold the pet, the mother will protect her child, and the man will sacrifice his life to protect all three. This is natural biology—the man and woman want to ensure their offspring survive. Men who give their lives for their families are considered heroes, but this does not negate the fact that a man's life is considered disposable as long as his death is for the "greater" good.

This is one of many reasons why men are considered the "real" romantics. Most men have a romantic sense of love with a woman they are pair bonded with. They want to believe in the fantasy of having a fulfilled life— sexually satisfied, loved, respected, and appreciated by a woman. The cold, hard truth is that he is only given those things for *what* he is, never who he is. Remember utility. As Rollo states, "The grand design of women's Hypergamy that men believe it is women who are the romantic ones."[14]

Men want to believe in the romanticism of true love and ignore the fact that women love opportunistically. Men are unable to tell when a woman no longer loves them, and when men experience a woman blindsiding them as she leaves the relationship, they don't understand the why. It's cold and calculated and has been reenacted in a woman's mind over and over again for months before the actual breakup occurs. Remember that women initiate divorce 80 percent of the time, often making themselves single mothers when they leave.

John experienced how inundated the modern sexual marketplace was with single mothers. Profile after profile of postwall women, overweight women, sugar babies, feminists, and single mothers saturated the marketplace— each with her own story, of course. This was John's online dating reality.

John observed women writing dating ads listing the qualities defining their perfect idea of a good man. On average, they wanted a tall (over six feet), educated (more educated than they), fun (must do things to entertain her), handsome, financially (at least six figure salary) secure man who had a great personality, had his shit together, and was looking for a serious relationship.

Despite having listed all these desired qualities in the other, the women seldom wrote ads listing qualities that a man would be interested in. Again, feminism has taught women not to do anything for the expressed pleasure of a man. From a high-status male point of view, when women sexualize themselves on dating apps, it shows they really only have their body to offer a man and nothing of intrinsic value. This is fun for short-term sex but negates any long-term potential because the sex is so freely given.

Remember, women will break rules for Alphas and make rules for Betas. Other men of lower status would have to jump through hoops for that which was freely given to John by so many women. They would have to earn the sexual intimacy that was given to John and so many men before him. A woman's sexual past is and typically always will be a trove of hidden secrets. The Alpha brings out her primal sexuality, while Beta men get duty sex. The Alpha is the one she pines for; the Beta is the one she settles for. Let that sink in.

A woman can only be picky when she has all the options and traits a man is looking for. If she does not have any of the traits men want in the long-term, she is only as valuable as the three holes she can offer him. You cannot turn a ho into a housewife, and a woman who has been with a multitude of men (riding the cock carousel), unable to pair bond with her man, is not a good long-term prospect or investment for any man. When a man is thinking about entering a long-term relationship, he should always ask these questions: If you took sex out of the equation, how would the woman complement your life? Does she detract from your goals? What else does she bring besides sex?

With a plethora (thank you, *The Three Amigos*) of single mothers on the dating market professing how their children always come first, you have to dissect this statement for what it is. Although you should never take at face value what a woman says and always observe what a woman does, let's take a closer look at how her children come first. At the basic level, sex occurred with an Alpha to produce children, satisfying her sexual imperative. Now as a single mother, she is looking for the Beta provider to offer long-term security for her and her children.

A single mother will absolutely have the hot, kinky one-night stand sex with an Alpha. She will even use sex as a tool to secure a Beta into a commitment. A perceived Alpha is her priority, and she knows in her mind he is only useful for her short-term sexual strategy. When she has secured a Beta with sex, hypergamy knows it will pay dividends to her and her children in the long term.

When dating a single mother, you will never come first—ever. This is why you can never date or have a long-term relationship with a single mother. You will always be last on the totem pole. You're not much of a priority to her compared to dating a single woman without children. When assuming the role of stepfather, you are in essence being cuckolded. You are raising another man's children. Those children do not see you as their "real" father, they do not carry your DNA, and, unless adopted, they will not carry your last name. In addition, depending on your state or local laws, once you have established a relationship where you are viewed by the children or state as a parent, you can be held financially responsible for child support. Even for children who are not biologically yours.

What single mothers are looking for are Beta providers. They are looking for someone who is financially secure and reliable and someone whom they can extract resources from for themselves and their children. For example, if you are dating a single mother and you eventually meet her children, it's no longer you and her. You are using your financial resources to lavish upon her and her children dinners, activities, and vacations. You are now providing your resources to children who will never be biologically yours (i.e., you are now a Beta provider).

The concepts of Alpha and Beta are not meant to be derogatory, but, for the purposes of this chapter, they provide an oversimplified sociological tier system to illustrate how women perceive men. Are you perceived as a leader or a follower? Do you command a room or blend in? Do you put women on a pedestal and put a woman's needs before your own? Would you willingly lay your life down for women and children because it's the right thing to do? Asking yourself hard questions and being honest with yourself are the only ways to truly understand who you are. Many men and women cannot look at themselves in the mirror because they do not like the answers.

John had to answer these very same questions to truly understand himself—change what needed to be fixed, love himself, be unapologetic for who he was, and make the changes to be the man he envisioned himself to be. A positive side effect of a man who lives an authentic life is men want to be him, and women want to be with him. It's raw, authentic, and genuine. It's something perceived as rare because a man who is comfortable with himself by himself, who is confident and independent, is the man both men and women want to be associated with.

One of the harsh realities of modern dating is that the use of social media and the resulting interconnections between everyone have changed the dynamic of how men and women interact. Interpersonal relationships are only a click away, don't require emotion, and are disposable. If one relationship fails, it's quite easy to find another person, again just a click away. The cold and callous nature of online dating and social media play a large part in how we interact and has resulted in profound disconnection.

"Ghosting" is becoming a common term in the modern age of social interaction. Men and women who have experienced modern online dating have had several experiences of ghosting and may have ghosted other people themselves. John certainly did this and stopped when he had it done to him. The sudden cutting off of contact with another person without so much as a consideration for the other person is emotionally unintelligent. If John wasn't interested in someone, he would be upfront—not only ensure there was clarity to what he thought and felt but not string a person along or perpetuate an emotionally damaging cycle.

Often times men don't understand that the medium is the message. Ghosting from her end? The medium is the message.[15] She is not interested in you. Flaking on a date? The medium is the message. When a woman appears to be "into" you and then suddenly goes cold? The medium is the message. The behavior of a woman, whether she has weak or strong interest in you, is the message. A woman who is interested in you and has genuine desire for you will make it abundantly clear she is into you. Receiving mixed signals from a woman? The medium is the message. This means she is debating whether you are a good prospect based on her hypergamous filter, and she does not genuinely desire you.

There is no mistaking a woman's genuine desire, and when a woman does have genuine desire, she will never engage in any behavior perceived as risky or comprise her status with the man in question. Men and women communicate in two very different ways. Men communicate overtly (direct and with logic), whereas women communicate covertly (indirect with feeling). Her communication is based on her feelings and how she feels in that moment.

This is a point of contention and frustration between men and women because not only do they compete with differing sexual strategies, but they also communicate in completely different manners. For men it is important to understand, not only hear, what a woman says; it is imperative to see what a woman does. The medium is always the message.

Men communicate to convey information, prioritizing content, while women convey context and feeling. John and millions of other men think women communicate rationally with an inclination toward analytic problem-solving, thus continuing to perpetuate the myth that men and women are equal in how they communicate. This cannot be further from the truth. Yes, women have the ability to be problem solvers; however, it is not within their innate feminine communication style.

Men should always be observant when openly communicating with women. Men need to have patience, which many men do not have. Women are masters at covert communication. What may appear to be a childish form of communication because it's indirect and inefficient compared to how men overtly communicate is actually the emotional reaction to their environment. This also perpetuates the myth that women are mysterious (the feminine mystique) and can never be figured out. This myth provides women plausible deniability for a lifetime.

There is nothing more frustrating for a woman than to communicate with a man who just doesn't "get it." When a man just doesn't get it, a woman will resort to overt communication because clearly her covert communication is not working. The man is either not receptive or he is unobservant about what she is trying to communicate. It is widely joked that women are crazy. People laugh at this and socially accept this as a truth to some degree because there is always some truth behind a joke. Yes, women can be crazy, but as Rollo points out, it's a calculated crazy. Men have to be observant to understand the message, whether it is explicit or implicit.

John actively observed how the medium was the message while dating women online. Some women would ghost, some would just never answer his messages, and others would respond immediately. Understanding that the medium was the message and you cannot negotiate desire were invaluable to John's dating life. Women who didn't respond, had one-word responses (lack of desire), or were flaky on dates were ignored. John realized how to quickly weed those women out and move on to better prospects who showed genuine interest.

In the current modern dating market, men and women are all talking to multiple people at once. Men are competing against other men, just as women are competing against other women. Nobody ever directs their full attention to someone when there are so many options for men and women these days. Granted, women have a lot more options in the sexual marketplace than the majority of men.

The dating market has become skewed and imbalanced because it is the top-tier, above-average-looking men (SMV nine through ten) who have a wide array of options, while an average man who may be an SMV six through eight is less likely to have a lot of options. Comparatively, a woman who is an SMV four and a single mother has more options than an SMV-six-through-eight man any day.

As John continued to navigate the sexual marketplace, he observed a majority of the women were epiphany-phase career women who had put their careers first and were holding off on marriage/kids until they found their perceived "one" or soul mate. All thinking they had plenty of time to secure a high-value man. The same women who had ridden the cock carousel hard for ten to fifteen years, their fertile years, and now were ready to "settle down."

All these women had an expeditious timeline in which they *had* to meet a man, marry him, and hopefully pop out two or three kids by the time they were forty years old. Even women over forty still clung to the dream they would find a husband and have children before their fertility was gone, only to realize it was too late. Biology did not match with their timeline, often leaving them alone and miserable.

The feminist, gynocentric society we all now live in has done a disservice to men and women, while the current structure of divorce laws has effectively ruined both relationships between men and women and the institution of marriage as a whole. Women are consistently bombarded by social media, literature, and marketing ads propagating a fantasy that they can do anything a man can do but better. At the same time, men are represented as incompetent buffoons (e.g., Homer Simpson, Raymond in *Everyone Loves Raymond*; the list goes on and on). Take an objective look at any random modern TV series, movie, magazine article, Gillette razor ad—anyone?

The consistent and blatant devaluing of men has had severe consequences for boys and young men. They are taught from childhood that boys cannot be boys and anything they do as a boy is considered inherently toxic. Men who never show emotion or vulnerability are considered toxic. All the while if a man is in a relationship and consistently shows vulnerability, it is never seen as strength by a woman. A woman needs her man to be the "rock" in the sea of her emotions and feelings. If a man cannot be that, he is perceived as weak. It's certainly a Catch-22 when boys and men are brainwashed and chastised for not being vulnerable, but when they are, they are considered weak.

Women are fluid like water, and men are the container. Women hold the shape of that container until that container leaks. Showing lack of frame, vulnerability, or too much emotion all cause leaks in the container. Remember, men have to be strong no matter what. It does not matter if your dog has died, your parents have died, you have lost your job. As Billy Murray says in *Meatballs*, "It just does not matter." You may be able to get away with it if God forbid your child dies, but you better emote alone even in that case. You only get so many passes from a woman before her hypergamy kicks in and asks, *Is he really the best that I can do?*

John had learned from his childhood that it was best for him to not show vulnerability and to "bottle" things up as an act of self-preservation. He did not want to appear weak in front of his family or face the wrath of his stepfather. This idealism was reinforced in the Marines, where he was trained to show no pain. Pain is weakness leaving the body. In the police department, remaining calm and stoic answering calls for service required every ounce of self-control.

It was not that John didn't feel emotion; he processed it differently. Logic, reason, and then emotion. Whereas women typically process emotion, reason, and then logic. It's just another difference between how men and women process things. In the face of imminent danger, people look up to the man who can be stoic, logical, and reasonable, rather than someone who is going to lose his shit. In a situation where a man loses his shit while facing imminent danger, he becomes a liability to the woman's security. Security is a paramount survival mechanism for a woman's hypergamy.

If a woman cannot trust her man with her life, then he can never attain her love or respect. Her brain does not work that way. It's a biological imperative for a woman to know her man can provide security for her and her children. This is why women have vagina tingles and are attracted to men who have a propensity for violence compared to men who do not. This is why, for men, it is better to be the warrior in the garden than a gardener in war. Among many other traits required, this is another illustration of why men have the burden of performance.

There is a lot of discussion about what makes men Alpha or Beta. These are concepts that can either exemplify a man (Alpha) or be used as a belittling tactic (Beta). Alpha comes across as some imperial, revered, godlike status that all men wish for and strive to obtain. Beta men are viewed as predominately weak, providers, pushovers. Men want nothing more than to be considered Alpha men.

While men want to be an Alpha, women want to fuck them. James Bond, anyone? There is no empirical guide that leads men toward Alpha enlightenment. The concepts of Alpha and Beta are just placeholders to expand on thought processes and encourage more discussions about intersexual, intergender dynamics.

One woman can perceive you as Alpha while another woman perceives you as Beta. Circumstantial situations apply. Situational circumstances dictate what is perceived as Alpha versus Beta and how you react to them as they unfold. The same concept goes for work, relationships, social circles, and life. Life happens to everyone, and nobody gets out alive. That being said, there is no such thing as an Alpha female. A woman who has to act dominant is doing so because she has to provide for her own security.

If you are asking yourself whether you are acting like an Alpha or a Beta in a given situation, the real question you should be asking yourself is why you care about what other people think of you. What do you have to gain from other people's approval? Seeking validation from anyone, man or woman, is inauthentic and disingenuous. In such cases you are not living your life on your terms but trying to live up to conceptions of what other people think of you. This is especially true in the sexual marketplace. An Alpha male's indifference is more desirable when he does not qualify himself to women, whereas a Beta male who feels the need to qualify himself to women could not be more unattractive.

Growing up, John certainly felt he needed to qualify himself to his stepfather and mother. He sought validation from his parents in order to feel good about himself. It was when he learned to take control over himself, his actions, and his thoughts that everything changed. At that point he didn't know Alpha or Beta was a "thing"; to him it was simply the right thing for him to do. He learned through his accomplishments that making himself his own mental point of origin and the internal validation he received as a result far outweighed anything anyone would have been able to give him externally. He had a drive and a purpose. His mission, not other people, fueled his drive, and this served him best.

John had to learn to live life on his own terms and hold himself accountable for his actions. He was the author of his life path, no matter what life threw at him. This is where there is a divergence between Alpha and Beta men. Alpha men are always their mental point of origin. Beta men allow others to be their mental point of origin (codependency). Alpha men are strong, dominant, and confident because they have a clear focus and mission of what they want for themselves and are unapologetic about it. Beta men don't have a clear focus or drive; they lack dominance and confidence because they don't know what they want out of life. It's like being rudderless, with no direction.

Alpha men are willing to walk away or cut away people who do not complement their purpose. Beta men are too codependent and afraid of people walking away from them. Alpha men are stoic, while Beta men wear their hearts on their sleeves. Alpha men lead by example through action. Beta men follow the leader. Alpha men are direct and openly confrontational, whereas Beta men are typically nonconfrontational and passive aggressive. This is not the end all guide to what makes an Alpha man and a Beta man based on their perceived natures. This is more of a set of guidelines related to the differences between the two and an illustration of subconscious mind-sets and being.

Admittedly, John had grown up in a Beta mind-set based on the preconditioned teachings from his upbringing. This is more likely than not the case for millions of men because they are taught a certain idealistic way of how the world and women are without really knowing any better, thus taking this mind-set into the sexual marketplace. Things in reality seem to be off and at times at odds with what they were taught. This leads men like John down a path to figure out what is rational and seek answers as to why the teachings of their upbringing differ so much from reality.

Granted, a lot has changed in the sexual marketplace since our grandfathers' day. The "game" has changed thanks to technological advancements and social transformations. Men back then didn't have access to Red Pill information, whereas men today collaborate based on what they have collectively learned and experienced. Today there is a wealth of information for the inquisitive person at the touch of his fingertips.

The freedom and ease of access to information on a global scale is unprecedented, which has been a blessing and curse. Knowledge is power, and, to underline the point, not only has this knowledge given John invaluable insight, but he has become a better man for understanding how intersexual dynamics work from a mind-set separate from the feminine, gynocentric, socially implanted one.

CHAPTER 12

In late summer 2017, John once again had to deal with Amber in modifying a parental shared-custody agreement. He was still resolute in not wanting his sons Corey and Eric in contact with Amber's new convicted felon husband. It was nothing personal, but it was important for John to take care of his sons, and he didn't want anything bad to happen to them. After a long series of conversations, John begrudgingly acquiesced with very specific terms and conditions of how he would allow his children to visit their mother in Florida.

Because Amber had never paid any type of child support, she would pay for their round-trip plane tickets from Virginia to Florida. The boys were limited to supervised contact with her current husband and under no circumstances allowed to be alone with him. The holidays would be on a rotational basis. John or the boys were free to contact each other at any point during the boys' visitation with her. John didn't want to keep Corey and Eric from their mother, but Amber's lack of contact with the boys since the divorce had showed John that she really never cared about motherhood and that their sons had never been a priority in her life.

Even for the two years during which they were all living in Florida thirty minutes apart, Amber only visited the boys six times, including major holidays. Once John and the boys moved to Virginia, her only contact with them was via a phone call or FaceTime conversation for about an hour once a month. Amber never offered to help John provide school supplies, clothing, toys, and the like. The burden of their welfare was strictly on his shoulders as she had married a convicted felon and chosen to be a stepmother to his baby.

Once the agreement was reached, John continued to work and provide for his children. Having seen what the dating market was like, he focused more on his sons than seeking a potential mate. The time and effort he had put into dating had yielded no positive results, just a lot of sex with dozens of women who showed no real potential as serious partners. The sexual marketplace was too inundated with single mothers and heavily tattooed, heavily pierced, shorthaired, pink-haired women who all bought into the feminist narrative (i.e., modern-day Western women). All of these women presented more red flags than a Chinese Communist parade. Frankly, knowing his own value in the sexual marketplace, he was not going to fall into another future train wreck.

The juice was not worth the squeeze and certainly not worth his continued investment. Focusing on his sons, his career, and his goals was more personally fulfilling than having sex with some postwall feminist. At least he would be able to see the positive returns from investing in his children over dealing with relationships. This is where John could understand MGTOW. Most of these men have either experienced or observed how men literally lose everything when a relationship collapses. He did not want to experience that again and certainly didn't want to expose his sons to it.

In the Red Pill community, there is a lot of discussion of MGTOW—many questions regarding whether MGTOW is the correct answer to solving the disparity between men and women. Yet it's really up to the person to decide what is best for his life and his personal goals. It's a compelling argument for men to no longer want to play the "game" with women and dating. Men are in an era never seen before in human history.

Men can be accused of sexual harassment in the workplace for complimenting a woman, holding a door open for a woman, or having a conversation that is overheard and taken out of context. Staring at a woman for longer than five seconds can be considered sexual assault. False rape allegations and #MeToo have become mainstream.

It's a very fine line for men, who can lose their careers, livelihood, and, in extreme cases, their freedom from a false accusation. Yet women constantly wonder, where have *all* the good men gone? Men who have become Red Pill aware or have too much to lose realize this is the new environment they have to operate in. For men it has become dangerous and a liability to interact with women. One false perception on a woman's part can literally ruin a man, a fact reinforced by the current legal system and social climate. This is why men are moving toward MGTOW in droves. They are refusing to play the game, and objectively they are doing what's best for them.

Thus men like John have begun to wake up and either take a break from or completely exit the sexual market-place. With conversations and consensual intimate encounters having to be documented as evidence for fear of future false accusations based on women's regrets, men live in a state of fear, navigating the minefield of inter-sexual dynamics. The transfer of power has been given to women since the legal system and corporate human resources will always side with a woman, unless there is blatant evidence to the contrary of their accusations. And still the man will face repercussions.

The inequity and bias against men in the system as a whole further illustrate this point. Men in relationships and marriages are still held 100 percent accountable and responsible (burden of performance) with 0 percent authority, authority now having been transferred to women and the "state."

If the man does not continue to perform, or the woman is unhappy for any reason that involves or does not involve the man, the woman is free to leave that relationship and is rewarded for leaving with alimony, child support, and state assistance. Women are now monetarily incentivized to leave relationships, since they have the power of the state to support them.

The "war on men" has increased immensely over the last couple decades. It started with representations of men as incompetent buffoons and has moved onto call for all-out war on the "patriarchy" by women. It is now mainstream and socially acceptable to degrade, shame, and undervalue men as a rule. Masculinity and the patriarchy are considered toxic and evil.

Young boys are taught to hate themselves for being boys. The growing number of young men checking out of society is evidenced by women now surpassing men in graduating with bachelor's degrees and women comprising more of the workforce. Objectively, women are now "slaves" to corporate America.

There is now a lost generation of men who will grow up not knowing what it is like to be a man because it has been socially ingrained in their psyche to hate masculinity. Guess who will be blamed for this? Men will be, of course, because they are not "stepping up." Lost generations of men will be blamed because women will now "suffer" as they are unable to find a suitable partner who is comparable or better on the dating market. Whether we choose to accept it now or later, masculinity is dying.

Recognizing this, John showed his sons that it was good to embrace their masculinity, that is was OK to be a boy and grow into a strong, competent, confident young man, a rarity these days. Although they were very stressful at times, the best years of John's life consisted of being with his sons, just the three of them. They had a strong father-son bond, one that seemed unshakeable; he could not have been happier with them in his life. They were his world, and he was theirs. Up to this point, John had lost everyone who had ever been close to him in his life.

He only had his sons and himself left in this world, and he could never imagine losing them.

Two weeks before Christmas 2017, based on his court agreement with Amber, John sent the boys down to Florida to spend the holidays with Amber and her family. This was the first time John wouldn't share Christmas and New Year's Eve with the boys. Although it was nice that he had the place to himself for once, he missed them dearly. On Christmas Eve, John received a call from Amber, who was frustrated Corey was not behaving well; she claimed she was going to cancel his Christmas. After John had a long discussion with Corey and Amber, Corey enjoyed his Christmas, although John could tell Corey was unhappy being there.

The boys' two-week visit with their mother came to an end a couple days after New Year's Day. John picked the boys up from the airport, and he noticed Corey and Eric now dressed and looked very different than the boys he had sent down to Florida. They each gave John a hug, and he was incredibly happy to have them back home. He was excited to be able to spend time with them, although something inside John told him there was something wrong. He couldn't put a finger to it, but he was aware there was a very apparent change in his sons.

A few days later, a large snowstorm rolled in, canceling the schools in the area. Corey, being a very responsible twelve-year-old young man, was trusted by John to watch over Eric while he was at work. There were very strict rules his sons had to adhere to. First and foremost was understanding their emergency plan and whom to contact in case of an emergency. No using the stove, keep the phone within arm's reach so John would call every hour to check on them. Their premade lunches were in the refrigerator, and they were to complete the preassigned homework John had given them to work on. John trusted his sons immensely and had no cause for worry in leaving them alone for a couple hours.

When John had finished work and was starting his car to head home, there was a message for him to contact social services. He returned the call and was advised that he needed to meet with a social worker and a sheriff's detective at the local station. They needed to have a conversation about the boys. John asked if they were OK, his heart beating fast. He was advised they were fine. John's mind was racing as he drove to the police station. His previous police experience told John that he was now under investigation, and he instinctively knew that this was not going to end well. What John did not realize was the fact that his whole life was about to change forever.

John arrived at the sheriff's station and waited for several minutes for the detective and the social worker to arrive. When they arrived, John was escorted back to an interview room where they would discuss with John what was going on. Because of John's previous police experience, he knew what was happening and automatically went into internal preservation mode. He knew he should not answer any questions because they would be used against him in any future proceedings, which John knew were imminent. He knew he was going to be arrested and was going to jail that night.

[Note: This is not professional legal advice and always consult an attorney regarding legal matters.]

John knew based on experience that if you are ever detained and questioned in a criminal legal matter against you, you must never, ever, under the pain of death, answer any questions posed by law enforcement without an attorney present. Anything you say will 100 percent, absolutely be used against you. It's even written and spoken when you are read your Miranda rights.

You can never fight your case in an interview room because the police already know what your fate is going to be for that evening. The only way to defend yourself is in the court of law with an excellent attorney on your side. What many people don't fully understand is that when you answer the detective's questions in a criminal case against you, you are not helping yourself. You are only strengthening the case against you.

Law enforcement officials will tell you how to help yourself and any number of psychological tactics for how to answer their questions. Always seek an attorney before answering their questions. Remember, the burden of proof is on them to prove to the court you are guilty beyond a reasonable doubt. If you think you are helping yourself out, once again, you are not. You are only making it easier for them to prove your guilt, even if you are guilty of whatever offense you are being charged with.

John remained silent as he was asked if he had spanked his kids the night before, advising the detective that he was not going to answer any questions without a lawyer present. John asked the detective what had transpired for them to warrant going into his home and interviewing his children without him present. The detective advised John that his children had told Amber they had been spanked and left home alone, which is not illegal in Virginia. Deputies responded to John's residence with a social worker. There the boys were subsequently interviewed, and it was determined there was probable cause for John having committed domestic assault for spanking his children.

John remained silent, and the detective realized he was not going to provide any information. The detective advised him to stand up and that he was under arrest for two counts of domestic assault for spanking his sons. As the cuffs tightened on John's wrists behind his back, he accepted his fate for now. He knew the situation was out of his hands. He could not believe he was being arrested for domestic assault for spanking his sons. John knew in the back of his mind that somehow Amber was behind all of this.

After John was searched and his personal items bagged, he was escorted to the back of the station to a waiting police cruiser. John was right about the sheriff's department already knowing what they were going to do with John. For the second time in his life, John was heading to jail. He felt mostly numb about what was happening, thinking about his career and livelihood now being in jeopardy. Knowing it was out of his hands, he knew the only way to fight this was to hire an excellent attorney.

Upon his arrival at the detention center, the same interviewing detective met John as he arrived in the receiving area of the jail. Having transported hundreds of people to jail during his law enforcement days, John knew the drill. Before speaking with the magistrate, the interviewing detective once again asked John questions about the incident. John keeping his mouth closed. He was taken before the magistrate to determine whether or not he should be remanded into custody or be released on bond.

The magistrate asked John personal questions; the warrants were obtained and signed before him. John was released on a personal recognizance bond and issued an emergency protective order (EPO). The EPO prevented him from having any contact with his children, and he had to relinquish his firearms and ammunition to a friend until the matter was cleared up. The whole process took about two hours.

Upon his release John was able to call one of his close friends to pick him up from the detention center. On the drive home, John spoke candidly about the whole incident. Walking inside his eerily quiet house, silent in the absence of sons, and shaking, John crawled into bed with the covers over him in shock at that evening's events. He didn't know what was going to happen to him. Although he knew in his heart he had done nothing wrong, he also knew he had to notify his work about the incident because of his level of government clearance.

Returning to work the next day, John advised his management and company security, apprising them of the situation that had transpired the evening before. Although facing two counts of domestic assault would not necessarily end John's career and terminate his clearance, if convicted, he would never be able to possess a firearm or ammunition ever again. The team he worked on was very supportive, especially his best friend Markus Wright, with whom he had been friends for a couple years. Markus had always been there for John.

Markus always had a clear and logical thought process, and John had always valued Markus for his friendship, insight, and almost superhuman logical reasoning. Markus had already experienced and seen what John had gone through, his life experiences seeming almost incommensurate with his age. They both knew John was in a shitty situation and realized the seriousness of the ramifications pending the outcome of the criminal proceedings.

Thursday evening, two weeks after his arrest for domestic assault, John was about to head to bed when he heard the doorbell ring.

Who could be at the house this time of night? he asked himself.

As he opened the door, three sheriff's deputies stood in front of the doorway.

"Are you John Devereaux?" one deputy asked.

"Yes, sir, I am John," he replied.

"You are under arrest," the deputy stated as they entered his house and grabbed John's wrists. Without resisting, John allowed the cuffs to be secured around his wrists.

"What am I being arrested for?" John questioned.

"We have two warrants for felony strangulation," the deputy responded.

"What? Are you kidding me? I didn't strangle anyone!" John exclaimed. In his mind, John thought, *What the actual fuck is going on?* He internalized his fear because he knew the serious ramifications of being charged with one, let alone two, felony offenses. He knew he was going to be spending some time in jail. How long could only be speculated at that point.

Once again he was searched, placed in the back of a police cruiser, and transported back to the detention center where he had been just two weeks prior. Internally shaking with fear, he remained calm and cooperative with the deputies as he once again was interviewed by the investigating detective. He saw the magistrate once again; because of the seriousness of the charges, John was remanded into custody, booked, and processed. He knew he was going to be there for a while. After the booking process was complete, John was able to contact his attorney and notify him of the situation.

John's attorney advised him that because he had been arrested on Thursday night, he would not be given a bond hearing until the following Monday. For the first time in his life, John was going to be spending the weekend in jail. He could not believe what was happening to him. This gave him considerable time to think about what he was going to do when he got out of jail—if he got out of jail. There was a real possibility he could remain in jail until his hearing date if he was not able to receive or post bond for the two felonies.

The first night in holding, John had to sleep in a cell for the first time in his life. He was not allowed to join the "population" for over forty-eight hours. The lights never went off for the entire period he was in holding. Sleeping on a two-inch-thick blue mat that did little to protect his bones from the metal slab, he lay there thinking about what was going to happen to him. Of course, he had been in worse situations in Iraq, but now he was being perceived as a criminal and contemplated how his life had changed forever.

The next morning John received a cellmate who would sleep on the floor as he remained on the bed. His cellmate was given a thicker mattress pad to compensate for sleeping on the floor. They discussed their cases and the circumstances around the fact that they were both in the same predicament. John never revealed his prior career in law enforcement. He had quickly developed a strong disdain for law enforcement and the criminal justice system as a whole.

After two days in holding, he was moved to B block in the detention center and housed with that block's population. His former receiving cellmate shared the same cell on B block. It was nice because they were familiar with each other and got along pretty well. John had seen many movie scenes and documentaries about jail and prison life. It was a whole other matter to be experiencing it in real life. He had the time to think about and strategize his case, develop primary and alternate plans for his life, and consider what paths were available to him.

John, having always felt alone, now felt more alone than ever. He missed his sons and hoped they were OK as he tried to fathom what the hell had happened. Going over everything in his mind, over and over again, he had all the time in the world with his thoughts. This was not a time to think irrationally; he had to keep his logic and reasoning intact. He was just counting down the hours until his bond hearing with the judge, hoping he would get a bond and get out.

At a snail's pace, Monday morning arrived. John was taken out of B block and waited in a row of seats for his turn to talk to the judge. During the opening arguments, the commonwealth attorney vehemently requested that the judge deny bond until the hearing. John's lawyer argued that John maintained a home in the county and had a steady job, as well as a previously exemplary record and no prior criminal charges deeming him a flight risk. The judge concurred with John's attorney, and his bail was set at $2,500 secured.

Time seemed to almost stop as John waited from Monday morning until later that afternoon before he was bailed out of jail by one of his close friends. When John arrived home after his weekend in jail, he secluded himself in his bedroom. Fear constantly lingered that he would hear another knock on the door; he was petrified that the police were going to arrest him again. As childish at it may sound, John found security under his blankets. The world around him was unable to penetrate the layers of cloth.

The next morning John got dressed in his usual business suit and headed into his office. He had to once again brief his work manager, his company management, and the security office about what had happened Thursday evening. Having provided the security office with all of the paperwork associated with his case, John was able to remain working until the case was settled. John also knew that even with one felony conviction he would lose his clearance. He was facing two felonies and two misdemeanors with the potential for twelve years' prison time.

John had never before contemplated what it would be like to lose his freedom, and for the first time truly understood how precious his freedom was. Walking in the halls at work, seeing the pretentious people walking with sticks shoved high in their asses—their arrogant thoughts that they were the most brilliant and most important people in the world only made John laugh on the inside.

As the days turned into weeks, and weeks turned into months, John still had had no contact with his sons. His trial date was set and rapidly approaching. John's attorney advised him of the evidence against him. Although there were no marks on Eric from the spanking, there was a small one-inch mark on Corey's butt. That answered the domestic assault charges; John questioned how he was being charged with two felony strangulation offenses.

John's attorney advised him that after the boys were removed from the home, they underwent a medical evaluation. It was there the boys claimed John had choked them over a series of a couple months before their Christmas vacation at Amber's. Pictures were taken to illustrate how they had been choked. John was floored, to say the least.

"What are they talking about? I taught them self-defense, and never have I ever choked them," John exclaimed. "I taught my son's self-defense and how to avoid situations like that because it is important for them to know how to defend themselves. For God's sake, I was in the military and on the police force. How could I not make sure my sons knew how to protect themselves!"

"Look, John, I believe you," his attorney stated. "Even looking at the medical report, there was no signs of marks or internal bruising. The felony strangulation charges are going to be very hard for them to prove."

John replied, "I mean, for fuck's sake, if the children were being abused, the school nurse, who sees Corey every day for his medicine; their teachers, whom they work closely with; and Eric's day care provider would have recognized or seen physical signs because they are trained to do so." John just sat in the chair, a wide range of emotions brewing deep within, hopelessness and despair being the main, consuming feelings. This was a process he had to see to its conclusion.

Even with John's exemplary past in the Marines, as a police officer, and working for the government with the highest security clearance, he knew he didn't stand a chance in hell of winning this case. John knew the Virginia criminal justice system all too well. For whatever it was worth, John was going to attend his first hearing and decide what he was going to do next. He had to plan for every possible outcome.

As John continued to await his trial, he talked extensively with Markus about his case and what legal avenues to pursue. One day in particular, as John and one of his friends conversed in the hallway, he noticed a woman at work whom he had previously seen before when he had walked the halls. John approached her and introduced himself. There was something about her that drew him to her. John asked for her name so he could messenger her on the computer later. She smiled and introduced herself as Samantha Santoro.

When he returned to his computer, John messaged Samantha. They began chatting and found out they had a lot in common. He was not pursuing her romantically, not only because of what he was personally going through but also because she worked in the same building as him, she was married, and John had been able to tell immediately she was a genuinely kind person. They became very close friends very quickly.

John and Samantha began talking and taking walks together every day. They learned more about each other with every interaction. The only flaw in her personality was her absolute love of olives. With John looking past her terrible taste in olives, their bond grew stronger and John's trust in her grew deeper, which is shocking because John had had astounding trust issues with people up to that point. Until John met Samantha, he had only trusted Markus, and with each passing day, John, Markus, and Samantha became very close friends.

With his trust in Samantha cemented, John explained everything that had happened to him over the past couple months. Instead of judging him, she was there to listen to John as he explained away what he had been going through. She supported John, and he knew he could rely on her like he could Markus to get through this very tough time. For any person going through such a stressful time, having a strong support network is vital, no matter the outcome.

As John's trial date drew closer, the stress began to consume him. One night, alone in his house, he sank into a dark place. This place was familiar to him because he had been there twice before. Once again, the thought of ending his life consumed his thoughts. He had spoken with Samantha; her instincts could tell there was something very wrong. With the prospect of attaining freedom and once again being zeroed out, John mentally planned his suicide.

Midway through his mental planning, John began to think about what his death would really accomplish. It wouldn't give him his kids back, and it was a response to a temporary situation. This was where, once again, Red Pill understanding and his love for himself, his children, and his closest friends were able to bring light to a dark situation. John understood that suicide was used by some to build themselves up. You would always be remembered by a select few but largely forgotten in time.

John recognized that if he went through with it, Amber and the courts would automatically think he was guilty of the crimes he was charged with, and for him that was completely unacceptable. He still didn't care about what people thought of him; however, he deeply cared about how he thought of himself. Suicide would be giving up in the face of adversity, and he was certainly no quitter. In his mind one measure of a man was what he did in the face of adversity. Did he buckle, or did he fight back?

Realizing he had more fight in him, he chose to pursue the best course of action to preserve himself, his career, and his livelihood. If he was going to go down, it was going to be on his terms and nobody else's. Embarrassed for even contemplating such a horrible thing again, John knew he was stronger than that. If he could get past this, there would be nothing in the world that could ever lead him to contemplate suicide again. Red Pill teaches men that if they have the drive, they can always rebuild their lives, making men better and stronger for having experienced their own personal adversity.

The trial date arrived, and the evidence was heard. The medical professional who evaluated the boys admitted that he observed no damage to the children's throats. Inconsistent with being strangled. It was also learned that Amber had played mental games with the boys since the first day they had arrived in Florida and throughout their entire time visiting her over Christmas. She had interrogated her children for fresh information about John and his life, going as far as to ask the boys if they wanted to live with her and not live with John. Amber had also contacted child protective services days before John ever spanked the boys. And she had coerced Corey into contacting the child abuse hotline to say he was being abused; this was heard via recording when Corey was on the phone with Amber as he answered the social worker's questions. The social worker went so far as to cut off the recording momentarily before resuming. The children were interviewed, photographed, and removed from the home without John having any knowledge of what was going on.

John learned that the boys had been in foster care since early January. Amber was very angry with the courts because they had not allowed the boys live with her down in Florida. Yet, because her husband was a three-time felon, both Virginia and Florida agreed it was in the best interests of the children to remain in the Virginia foster care system. This is where his sons would remain for over a year because Amber would not divorce her husband and move him out of the house.

Based on the totality of the evidence and testimony heard in court, John had concluded that Amber's goal was to ruin him, using the legal system, which typically favors women, against him. Once John was ruined and convicted, she knew he would lose custody of the boys. She also knew he would lose his clearance (a.k.a. career), home, and livelihood, and she would retain full custody of the boys, so John would have to pay her child support. The one thing she never thought through was how her relationship would affect the boys being able to live with her. The boys had been used as pawns in a game they didn't understand.

John was never angry with his sons. He was furious at the fact that their mother would use her own children against their father in a way that would permanently damage them. It was clear she only cared about herself and, as her past had indicated, she never considered the emotional and psychological toll she would inflict upon her own sons. Just to get back at John. Something he would never forgive her for. His close relationship with his sons effectively severed.

With his first trial concluded, John had a very candid conversation with his attorney. They both knew John was never again going to gain custody, and even if by some miracle he won the case and retained custody, child protective services would maintain a watchful eye on him and his children. Although this was not a problem, the fact that Amber was willing to go to such great lengths to ruin John was. He concluded it would only be a matter of time before Amber pulled another stunt like this.

Creating a criminal defense matrix, John had to be practical about the situation before him. He had to triage what was important to him and base his defense on how he was going to move forward. Acting out of self-preservation, John knew he had to protect himself and his career first. Without his career and clearance, he would be unable to sustain his livelihood. He also had to protect himself from Amber and any future attempts on her part to interfere with his life. He needed her out of his life once and for all. As for his sons, he knew there was no way to get them back.

Knowing there were only certain legal avenues to pursue, John, in making *the* hardest decision of his life, chose to give up his parental rights to his sons. By doing this, he would no longer have a need for Amber in his life, thus mitigating any future liability regarding his clearance and career. Knowing they only had unreliable and tainted testimony, combined with the lack of any physical evidence, the commonwealth offered John a plea deal, under which if John plead guilty to the two misdemeanor domestic assault charges, the felony charges would be dropped. He would serve ten days in jail, and one year of probation, and attend a nine-month domestic assault course, and his termination of parental rights would be approved.

Looking at the terms of the plea deal, John was confident the two misdemeanor convictions would not affect his clearance. Because the felonies were dropped, he decided that this was going to be the best course of action for him. He was assured this plea would preserve his clearance and his career. Based on John's experience in law enforcement, he understood that unless you have been involved in the criminal justice system, law enforcement and the state will add as many charges as possible to your case, knowing this will put them in a better position to offer a plea deal (wherein often times they will drop the charges on which they can't get a conviction).

What matters is that the defendant pleads guilty to some of the charges. Not only does this allow law enforcement and the state to save face, it also allows the commonwealth or state's attorney to get the conviction. A commonwealth or state's attorney is less likely to get promoted over another candidate if the other candidate has a higher conviction rate. So, with every conviction they receive, the attorney's career is bolstered, and John's case was no exception.

After much deliberation, John signed the plea deal. He didn't have the money for a full-blown jury trial, and he had been assured he could keep his security clearance. As he signed, he was in essence signing away his children, his exemplary record, his second amendment rights for life, and his dignity. John went before the same judge who had originally given him bond on the felonies, the same judge who had benched the civil portion of the trial, and the same judge who had benched his criminal trial; she approved the plea deal. Since the same judge had presided over the whole process, he knew there was going to be no impartiality on her part in future criminal proceedings.

Once the plea deal had been accepted, John was advised by the court that he could still not have contact with his children, even one last time. It had been four months since he had seen or talked to them. He was once again remanded into custody to serve the ten days' jail time. He was serving misdemeanor jail time, which was half of felony jail time. So, because John had been sentenced to serve ten days in jail, he only had to actively serve five days. And because he had already served four days, he would spend the night in jail only to be released in the morning. This was John's fourth time going to jail.

John was released the next morning. With a criminal record for the first time in his life, he took an Uber home and prepared his suit for work the next day. He hoped that everything had been resolved criminally; he now had to focus on salvaging his career and paying out of pocket for the assault classes and the court costs.

Although John's perception of the criminal justice system was forever skewed, he still wanted to serve his country.

Now having been on both sides of the criminal justice machine, he understood exactly why recidivism was incredibly high. Once people are convicted of a serious criminal offense, they are kept in the system by design. If they can't pay their fines, they go to jail. If they can't afford an attorney—sure, they get a court appointed one—they more than likely end up in jail. Failure to pay for the classes—they go to jail. Failure to abide by probation—they go to jail. It's an incredible money-making machine if you look at it objectively.

The only reason John was able to break the cycle was because he had a good job that paid well, so he was able to keep up with the payments to prevent reincarceration. If he failed any conditions of the plea or his probation, he would serve one year behind bars. John felt guilty of ever being a part of the criminal justice system. Something he was eternally ashamed of. When he was a police officer, he hadn't had any sympathy for those who broke the law, thinking they should pay the consequences.

Granted, it is a valid perception, and anyone who breaks the law should pay their dues, but he now understood firsthand that the criminal justice system is broken. Not only is the person still punished after having served his time; it's a lifetime punishment, with the lack of job opportunities, housing, and constitutional rights and a social stigma that never goes away. There is no real rehabilitation from the criminal justice system, because once you are in the "system," the cards are stacked against you, and it takes a near-herculean effort to stay out of it.

CHAPTER 13

John began to rebuild his new life as a single man, no longer a single father. It was time for him to start another new chapter in his life, this time without the children that he loved so much. Aside from Markus and Samantha, John was now alone. Starting over in a new life was not very easy for him. It was a dramatic lifestyle change, but he knew he had to make the effort to move on. He thought about his sons every day, and his heart ached to see and talk to them again. Every time he came home, a silent reminder of what once was surrounded him, his sons now only alive in his memory.

John logically knew he had made the right and reasonable decision in terminating his parental rights, but that did not detract from the pain he felt. He relived the happy memories with his sons, the trips and vacations they had shared, the adventures, the good times and the bad (which in retrospect weren't that bad at all). He missed their company, playing with them, teaching them, and being a father to them. They were his world, and now they were gone.

Regaining a focus on himself, he now had the time and "freedom" to build himself and his life back up. Amber had nearly ruined him with her premeditated actions. Now that she was completely out of the picture, John was finally free from her and her bullshit after all these years. It had just come at an extremely high cost to him and to his boys, who no longer had their father in their lives. John hoped that his sons would remember what they had been taught and never forget to focus on themselves, strive to be the best version of themselves, continue to pursue their dreams, and know that no matter where they were, John would love them until the day he died.

John was able to rebuild his life because of his Red Pill awareness. He knew from his previous experiences that no matter what, when all the chips were down, he had the knowledge and the skills to keep moving forward and had a half sleeve phoenix tattooed on his left arm to prove it. This served as a reminder to him that he would always be able to rise from the ashes. Life teaches us many hard lessons if we're aware enough of what is being taught. John had certainly learned an incredible amount about himself and his resilience in overcoming adversity; he had learned to always make himself his own mental point of origin and to always keep moving forward. John also knew that everything, *everything* in life is temporary.

Whether it is a situation, a career, home, family, or financial status—everything is temporary, and situations will always change; it's a fact of life. That is why it's important to enjoy the good times while they are here and use that time to prepare for the hard/bad times. Nothing will be bad forever, and nothing will be good forever. Enjoy the moments and growth when these trivial times are presented. There is an old Russian proverb: "The same hammer that can shatter glass can also forge steel."

The point being, live your life authentically. Step out of your comfort zone to learn and grow from every experience you can. John certainly had to, and it was painful, raw, and forever scarring. He became a better and stronger man for having had these experiences and overcome them. They had shown him how strong he was, how he would always persevere, and no matter what happened in life, he would continue to move forward and continue being the genuine and authentic person he was. Forevermore John was a new and changed man stepping forward into his new life.

The dating market remained the same, the difference being John didn't have his children this time. He kept his nice home, his career, even got a promotion into a senior level management position within his company. This was also when John decided that he did not want any more children. He could not and would not endure such pain again in his life, so he decided to get a vasectomy. John had learned from his mistakes and would never put himself in that position again. John would never date one woman exclusively; he was "plate spinning" postwall women in their thirties and forties, who would bring up their future plans of getting married and having children.

He would explain to them that marriage and children were not going to be in his future and that he would only have casual relationships. Some women accepted that, John knowing all too well that they accepted his decision for "right now," self-assured that he would change his mind later; others moved on because they didn't have the time to waste on their ever-ticking biological clocks (many were already past their expiration date as regards carrying healthy children).

In light of the shit show of dating and marriage today, it's understandable that a lot of men say, "Fuck it," and check out. John certainly had enough reasons to. The complementary nature between men and women is almost something of a bygone era and will seemingly never return. At least not any time in the near future. Right now, there is a power struggle between the sexes, and with the current "war on men and masculinity," men are increasingly responding with the MGTOW movement. You can't lose the game if you don't play the game; John understood why the MGTOW mind-set resonated with so many men and agreed with it.

Nature and biology never designed men and women to be at odds with each other. This is new territory, and both men and women are losing—miserable and uncomfortable in the presence of each other. From John's point of view, female nature has not changed. What has happened is social media and any number of movies/books have pronounced and magnified this behavior to negative ends. When combined with the imbalances in criminal/divorce laws and the now blatant and open bias against men, it is understandable that female nature is maximized, masculinity is minimized, and men want to stop participating in the game.

This begs the following questions. Do men and women want to address the elephant in the room and acknowledge a rift exists? How do we fix the rift between men and women? Can this rift be fixed, or does anyone really want to fix it? With very few exceptions (the Korean War, for example), in war there is a winning side and a losing side. What do women have to gain by winning the war on men? What do men have to gain by winning the war on women? No matter the outcome or which side wins, everyone will lose.

First and foremost, there needs to be a change in the draconian divorce laws that were created in a time during which intersexual dynamics were much different. The old divorce laws were instituted in a time when women stayed at home and raised children, while the men worked to provide for their families. There was balance, and these laws were created to help women in case the man left them and their children. Women typically didn't have any work skills because they did the domestic duties in the home. A divorce or a man leaving would be financially and socially disastrous for the woman.

The laws ensured that the man would be continually responsible for the welfare of the woman and child until a time when it was no longer necessary. In a way, these laws incentivized men and women to remain with their families, especially since they needed a valid reason to divorce. With the changes brought about by the sexual revolution and feminism, women no longer wanted to be the stay-at-home mom. They were experiencing their newfound sexual freedoms and beginning to work in corporate America, not to mention the fact that due to economic changes, households now needed two working parents to make ends meet.

Fast-forwarding forty-plus years, the relationships between men and women are very different. Now that there are no-fault divorce laws, men and women can file and receive a divorce for no reason at all. The disposability of relationships has never been worse. The only problem being that the man risks losing half of everything and needing to support any children in cases of divorce.

Women are incentivized to leave marriages, as evidenced by disproportionate number of women filing for divorce. As John's story indicates, they are awarded cash prizes and are supported by the government in doing so. The concept of marriage has now become a government contract between two parties, and when a divorce takes place, the man must pay or face additional legal and civil consequences. Modern marriage in Western society remains advantageous for women but has now become a liability for men.

Whether Western men choose to accept it or not, getting married to a modern, Western woman in our current society is one of the worst decisions he could ever make. If he is hell bent on getting married, he needs to be informed of national and state divorce laws and learn how to properly vet the woman. *But she won't ever do that to me; she loves me* is the typical response. You will never fully know who she really is until the day comes that you are on opposing sides of a courtroom. Right then and there, you will truly see her and how much she loved you as the state determines how much you get to pay her and how often you get to see your children. As a man, make your own well-informed decision about what is best for you and consider the 150-year marriage low in the United States, which speaks volumes.

John had concluded that he would never again marry a Western woman—and that was probably the best course of action for any man to take until the laws changed and became more balanced. Although John had gone MGTOW for a time to get his life back on track, it wasn't something he wanted to do permanently. John knew what was best for him and that was to do his own thing without any serious commitments. John still loved women and enjoyed their company from time to time, but they were never his focus, only complementary.

In the end each man has to make his own personal decision on what is best for him. The key is to make life-changing decisions while being well-informed, understanding the risks, mitigating the risks, and accepting that sometimes even if you have done everything right, that decision still may not work out well for you in the end. It's a fact of life. And in terms of decisions that do not work out in your favor, know that some just have more severe consequences; learn from the mistakes you made, brush yourself off, and continue to move forward.

Success for John was not only measured in accomplishments; success was measured in how many times he had been able to get up after being knocked to the ground. Failure and pain are some of the best teaching moments if we're insightful enough to be self-reflective and introspective and accept responsibility for our own actions. Accept responsibility for your shit, own it, learn from it, grow from it, and use it to better you.

Men of high value do not accept mediocrity in themselves and are always seeking ways to better themselves. Become the master of your life, and live it to the fullest extent possible. Take risks, get out of your comfort zone, learn new things, surround yourself with people who challenge you, enjoy yourself and being alone in your own company. You are in control of your life, and what you do with your time here is all on you and nobody else's responsibility. If you don't like something, make the change. Life is way too short to hold yourself back and not live life to the fullest.

In one scene of the movie *Braveheart*, William Wallace's charter profoundly states, "Every man dies; not every man really lives." This could not be more accurate, because years from now, lying on your deathbed, you will have plenty of time to think about what you might have been or could have done with your life. It's tragic to think how many men have died with the regret of not having done something significant with their life. Take a clear look at your life—are you where you want to be? What areas of your life can you improve? Are you pursuing your life's mission and goals?

John would certainly rather die young having experienced a well-lived life than live to be old having lived an unfulfilled one. When one goal or pursuit is reached, another is chosen. As Richard Cooper states, "Pursue excellence, not women"; this could not be more correct. Women will naturally gravitate to a man who is pursuing his mission and goals. Women do not want to be the center of a man's world, and no man should allow a woman to be the center of his world. If you are unsure about what direction you are going in, remember that your mission and goals will never tell you one day that they don't love you anymore.

It is a fact of life that you cannot place your life and existence in the hands of another person. One day this person will leave you either through choice or through death. This is why it is vital you are your own mental point of origin and live your life authentically for yourself. Women are complements and not the basis of a well-lived life. In the end it's up to you to make changes in your own life and do what's best for you. Just don't bullshit yourself or make any excuses as to why you can't make the changes you want.

Only you can effect change in your life; nobody else is going to do it for you. Just like it's your choice to take the Red Pill and accept uncomfortable truths or to remain in the Blue Pill paradigm. It's your choice to go MGTOW and check out if that is what's best for you or to take the chance on having relationships or getting married. Red Pill knowledge provides tools that you can either use or not, and what you do with them is all on you.

The Red Pill saved John's life. He was able to learn from the mistakes he had made and reinvent himself into the man he always wanted to be. He is still pursuing a lot of change and growth, and of course there will always be bumps in the road and setbacks, but that's part of the process. After having lived a very violent and troubled life, he has set himself back on track and continues to move forward in his new life with Red Pill awareness.

No matter what may be in John's future, he knows from his previous experiences that there is nothing that he can't handle, and no matter what adversity lies ahead, he is using the good times he is experiencing now to prepare for the bad. John's journey will continue. After all he is a Red Pill man rising from the ashes of his Blue Pill conditioning.

THE END

AUTHOR'S NOTES

Thank you for taking the time to read—and hopefully enjoy—my novel. This is a novel about self-discovery, perseverance, and knowing what information can literally save your life. I want to extend a personal thanks to Rollo Tomassi, Richard Cooper, Terrance Popp, Coach Greg Adams, and Joker from the Better Bachelor. You all have done a tremendous job in the Red Pill community, and your dedication is very much appreciated.

Growing up poor in a small, rural town in New York, I always wanted something more from my life. I had a thought in the back of my head that I was meant to accomplish great things and succeed, whereas other members of my family seemed comfortable in their way of life. I wanted more than to just survive. I wanted to live and experience all that life had to offer. I ask myself, *Did I live to my fullest potential? Did I live my life on my terms?* Looking back on my life, I see it's certainly had its ups and downs, like many lives, and I can honestly answer that I have lived one hell of a life and am grateful for all my experiences.

I also want to open a discussion about addressing some of the issues within our society centered on paradigms of men and women. Although some may think that the Red Pill community is misogynistic in nature, I think it's important we put bias aside for a moment and end the division between men and women. Men and women have so much potential when they work together as a team—not one side being better than the other, just complementary. Men and women are different from a biological perspective, and that is OK. Men and women also think differently, and that's OK too. But what is not OK is to elevate one gender above another.

As the Better Bachelor states, flip the script (which I personally agree with). If you have a statement that puts one gender above the other, flip the gender script in order to put things into a different perspective. It is not OK to put one race or religion above another, and it's not OK to put one gender over the other. Everyone deserves equality in opportunity from a humanistic perspective. Equality in outcome is up to each person to determine for themselves. You are responsible for what you do or don't do with your life.

To my sons, Colin and Ethan, I will forever love you, until the day I die. I think about you every day, and I miss you so much. You have so much potential, and I will always be there for you, no matter what. I sincerely hope one day I will have you back in my life and can see you develop into the strong, intelligent young men I know you will become. I love you boys, and whatever happens in life, I will always love you. You both are the best thing that has ever happened in my life.

I also wanted to give special thanks to Duane and Wendy. You both are amazing people, and my life is so much better with you in it. I value you both for the friendship, love, and support you have offered me in some of the hardest times of my life. I am truly blessed, and I am forever thankful I can share in your lives as you share in mine. The world is a better place with you two in it. With that, I'm out. Be kind, take care of yourselves, build yourselves up, and take charge of your life. It's never too late.

ENDNOTES

1 Tomassi, "Kill the Beta," The Rational Male, 2011. https://therationalmale.com/2011/11/21/kill-the-beta-2.

2 Tomassi, "The 5 Stages of Unplugging," The Rational Male, 2012. https://therationalmale.com/2012/07/25/the-5-stages-of-unplugging/.

3 Tomassi, "There Is No One," The Rational Male, 2011. https://therationalmale.com/2011/08/30/there-is-no-one/.

4 Tomassi, "There Is No One," The Rational Male, 2011. https://therationalmale.com/2011/08/30/there-is-no-one/.

5 Tomassi, "The Threat," The Rational Male, 2012. https://therationalmale.com/2012/02/10/the-threat/.

6 Tomassi, "Imagination," The Rational Male, 2011. https://therationalmale.com/2011/08/25/imagination/.

7 "Terminator Quotes," Quotes.net, accessed June 24, 2020. https://www.quotes.net/mquote/95506.

8 Robert Briffault, *The Mothers: The Matriarchal Theory of Social Origins*. New York: Macmillan, 1931, 21.

9 Tomassi, "Hypergamy Doesn't Care," The Rational Male, 2012. https://therationalmale.com/2012/05/16/hypergamy-doesnt-care/.

10 Tomassi, "Relational Equity," The Rational Male, 2017. https://therationalmale.com/tag/relational-equity/.

11 Tomassi, "Just Get It," The Rational Male, 2012. https://therationalmale.com/2012/08/22/just-get-it/.

12 Tomassi, "Iron Rules of Tomassi," The Rational Male, 2011. https://therationalmale.com/the-best-of-rational-male-year-one/.

13 Tomassi, "Rollo Tomassi: The Nine Iron Rules," The Rational Male, 2020. https://therationalmale.com/tag/rollo-tommasi-the-nine-iron-rules/.

14 Tomassi, "Men In Love," The Rational Male, 2017. https://medium.com/@RationalMale/men-in-love-a898dd127a65

15 Tomassi, "The Medium Is the Message," The Rational Male, 2011. https://therationalmale.com/2011/09/06/the-medium-is-the-message/.

Made in the USA
Monee, IL
22 January 2021